"I was hoping you'd ask me to stay,

for dinner, that is." Crew opened Alexia's refrigerator as he spoke. It yawned as empty as a school locker during summer vacation. "But I take it you don't cook much."

"Not from scratch," Alexia explained.

"Then you must eat out a lot," he said over his shoulder as he slammed the fridge shut.

"No, not really. I make good use of the can opener and microwave." Alexia paused and glanced up at Crew wickedly. "I do have two things I make from scratch, though."

Crew caught the naughty sparkle in Alexia's eyes. He leaned back against the fridge, his seductive body language challenging her to continue. "And what might they be?"

Alexia moved toward Crew as she slowly revealed her specialties. "Chocolate cake . . . and love."

Tiffany White's first Temptation, *Open Invitation*, had everyone talking. It was sexy—and fun. *Cheap Thrills* is even more fun *and* sexier! In fact, everything about Tiffany is outrageous—from her funky clothes to her wild tousled curls to her all-white home with the double bed just for Chloe the dog. Always provocative, always delightful, Tiffany's unique flair is best summed up in her motto, What do you mean, 'no'?

Tiffany, her wonderful husband and Chloe the dog live in St. Louis, Missouri . . . because it's fun.

Books by Tiffany White

HARLEQUIN TEMPTATION

274–OPEN INVITATION

Cheap Thrills

TIFFANY WHITE

Harlequin Books

TORONTO • NEW YORK • LONDON
AMSTERDAM • PARIS • SYDNEY • HAMBURG
STOCKHOLM • ATHENS • TOKYO • MILAN

For my editor,
VALERIE SUSAN HAYWARD,
who, like me,
marches to the beat of a different drummer....
Except she married into the band.

Published October 1990

ISBN 0-373-25418-0

Printed in U.S.A.

1

HANGING PRECARIOUSLY outside the fourth-floor window of an office building on a narrow piece of scaffolding washing windows was not Crew Harper's idea of a good time.

Although it was six o'clock in the evening, the merciless summer sun was showing no sign of heading for the horizon. With the back of his tanned wrist, Crew swiped at a trickle of sweat sliding down his temple. He was in the heart of yuppie land, and no doubt a cop would be along any minute to give him a ticket for sweating, he mused, certain there was some ordinance against it. With a wry chuckle he began finishing the last window for the day.

As he'd worked, he'd seen a steady stream of suits, both male and female, leave the gleaming glass-and-chrome office building he was working on and head for the parking lot and not home, but happy hour. Yuppies lived off the free food, since cooking took too much time away from their constant pursuit of achievement. At happy hour they could work the crowd as they ate.

Crew figured the building was empty and was just thinking about how good a cold beer and pepperoni pizza would taste when a sudden movement inside the office of the window he was washing caught his eye.

His attention was drawn to the sliver of open drapery to see a young professional woman finish stretching and rise from her chair, walking across the office to lock her door. Crew almost fell off the scaffolding when she turned and walked back toward her desk and began undressing.

The first article of clothing she removed was the wide brown crocodile belt she draped over the upholstered chair next to her desk. Then she gracefully kicked off her matching two-inch pumps.

A lump rose in Crew's throat when she began undoing the long white jacket she had belted over her slim skirt. A ray of sunlight glinted off her gold earring as she turned her head to look at the clock on the wall, and Crew's heart skipped a beat when he thought she'd spotted him. He could already hear the wailing sirens of the cops she would surely call if she caught him watching her. He let out a slow, shaky breath when he saw that he had escaped her notice.

Obviously working late, she was only getting comfortable, he decided, beginning to resume his work of washing her office window.

Except as he started to look away, she began unzipping her narrow skirt.

Damn!

No saint, he was compelled to continue watching her, all the while a little voice in his head was admonishing him for it. Normally he paid attention to the little voice, but he was hot, tired and thirsty. He deserved this harmless treat, he rationalized, muzzling his conscience.

And the woman . . . well, who could blame him. She was exquisite, even if she was a yuppie; the kind of woman he usually disdained. He liked his women more daring and individualistic. No, the cookie-cutter women, as he called them, with their leather brief-cases, power suits and appointment books scheduling their lives weren't his style at all.

Ambitious himself, he could understand their drive. He wasn't a chauvinist by any means, but what he couldn't understand was their willingness to sacrifice fun on the altar of career. Life was too short not to enjoy it.

The woman he was watching was as neat and sleek as her gray-and-mauve contemporary office, he noted as she padded across the carpet in her stocking feet. She hung up the skirt she'd removed on the hanger on the back of her office door. That finished, she stepped out of her snowy white half slip and was folding it when the telephone rang.

She turned and walked back to her desk to answer the phone, giving Crew a full view of her coltish legs beneath the hem of her long white jacket that barely skimmed the top of her sexy thighs. She laid the slip on the flame-stitched chair next to her belt and rested her hip on her desk as she took the call. Crew could see that her nails were long and manicured as she absently twisted her gold earring while listening to her caller.

The call was brief and when she hung up the phone she began walking back to the hanger on the door, her back to Crew as she slipped off the long white jacket.

Crew wiped his damp palms down his soft faded jeans that clung to him like the insistent urgings of his libido. His sleeveless white T-shirt was molded damply to his body. Things had reached the point at which he knew he should definitely stop watching, but he no longer could.

If he made any noise at all, the woman would know he was there. He was trapped hanging by a couple of ropes outside her window as he watched her hang up her jacket. Surely she was going to stop now anyway. She was down to next to nothing from what he could see from her back, just a wisp of a bra and . . .

She turned and he blinked. Those long, lean racehorse legs of hers were deceiving. She was lush on top. Her creamy breasts spilled over the top of a low cut, front clasp ivory-satin bra with lace insets.

Heady lust took over as he whispered, "Come on sweetheart, take it off. I can't stand it. Please, pretty please . . ."

She arched her back in a stretch and cupped her hand behind her neck, massaging out the kinks of a long day.

"Nooooo, don't tease me. . . . Take it off. P-le-eease. Come on, just for me, sweetheart."

His breathing was coming in small gasps and he was rock hard. Hell, he was human. No man could see something so beautiful and not respond, he reasoned.

As though she could hear his whispered urgings, she looked down and brought her hands up to unclasp the bra. Her breasts sprang apart, still sheltered in the silky cups of the skimpy bra, like fresh peaches wrapped in tissue.

"Mercy, I'm dying...no, I'm in heaven," Crew whispered inaudibly, his eyes heavy lidded with growing excitement. Nothing like this had ever happened to him before. Hell, things like this only happened in dreams...the kind of dreams you always woke up from too soon.

Her fingertips peeled away the scraps of wispy fabric, one side at a time, to reveal pink pouting nipples. Crew grasped the rope on the narrow scaffolding for balance. His fingers tightened until they were white knuckled as he watched her hands cup her breasts in gentle squeezes as if to ease away the tenderness from their day's constraint in satin and lace.

With a shrug of her smooth shoulders, she removed the bra completely and folded it on top of her slip. She paused for a moment, then seeming to hit upon some sudden inspiration, reached for a yellow legal pad and pen on her desk to jot something down, the action as she leaned from the waist causing her breasts to swing gently forward.

Crew groaned. He was definitely being punished for not listening to his little voice. It was too late now. No power on earth could keep him from continuing to watch the sensual sight unfolding in front of his disbelieving eyes. When the woman had leaned forward, she'd accidentally knocked over the glass of water on her desk, and then when she'd hurried to mop up the spill with tissues, her breasts had grazed the spilled water.

She had cleaned up the spill and now was dabbing the droplets of water on the tips of her breasts with tissue. Crew's mouth worked unconsciously...his tongue making licking motions, as his manhood strained against his ripped jeans.

When she had everything as neat as a pin again, she walked over beside her desk to toss the damp tissues in the waste can. Crew leaned sideways, away from the narrow slit between the drapery. When he leaned back, she was removing a soft canvas carryall from a tall white lacquer storage cabinet on the wall opposite her desk.

When she'd been undressing, he'd expected her to be wearing panty hose, and indeed she was, but these weren't like any he'd ever seen. They were a creamy shade with a lace top, the high-cut French panty accenting her shapely legs to stunning advantage.

She was one deliciously sexy yuppie, Crew thought. Too bad yuppies weren't his type.

Then, as he watched, she leaned forward to peel down the pretty panty hose, uncovering a thatch of caramel curls. She stood not six feet away from him wearing nothing more than her oversize glasses. His body throbbed insistently. Maybe he could make an exception...

Nah, he decided reluctantly. He didn't have time for romance right now. Getting the money to start his landscaping business was his main priority.

He had time for fun, yes, but not for the aggravation of trying to date a tunnel-vision career woman like her. She was extremely enticing—there was no question about that. But he didn't know a thing about her personality, and when it came right down to it, for him personality was the draw.

A sense of fun and adventure were as important to him as a lush body, and he hadn't seen anything about this woman to indicate either a sense of fun or adventure.

That is until she bent to unzip her canvas carryall.

"Well I'll be damned...." A wicked grin spread across Crew's face. He felt so hot he thought he might steam up the window he was supposed to be cleaning. For there, right next to the dimple on the woman's saucy bottom, was a tiny butterfly tattoo!

She was a yuppie, yes. But not your ordinary garden variety. It appeared a bit of a free spirit lurked hidden beneath the polished ambition. A free spirit Crew was suddenly yearning to set free. His mind tumbled over various ways to wrangle an introduction as the woman finished pulling on a shiny turquoise leotard over a pair of white capri tights, then tamed her short, adorably mussed curls back from her face in a banana clip.

She was obviously going directly from her office to work out, he surmised as he watched her take a pair of aerobic shoes from her canvas carryall. He supposed he could follow her to her gym and bump into her there. No, he was soaked with sweat and hardly wearing workout clothes. From the look of her, one had to dress the part. He wouldn't get past the front door in his torn jeans and T-shirt.

Meeting her would have to wait, but meet her he would. He didn't have any doubts about his ability to take it from there once he established contact. Women didn't intimidate him because he genuinely liked them.

As she slipped on her turquoise socks, he wondered just what it was she did for a living. Maybe there was a way to meet her using that angle....

His thoughts were interrupted when he saw the woman look up from tying her shoe laces to call out something in the direction of the locked door of her office. A few seconds later she opened it to admit a tall blond young man dressed in gym attire, who bussed her cheek as he entered.

So much for meeting her, he decided.

It seemed she was already involved with someone, though that certainly wasn't much of a kiss he'd given her. Maybe it was merely the way his type kissed. His type being the kind of man who didn't sweat, and if he did, it was only in designer sportswear.

It served him right, Crew decided, that she was already involved with someone. Watching her had not been one of his more shining moments of integrity, and he was beginning to feel guilty.

The young woman left her office—on a brief errand no doubt—and the blond man stayed behind to wait. Crew was about to start back to work, when the young man moved over behind her desk and began a search of its drawers. There was nothing necessarily strange about that if the two were intimate, but Crew thought it was an invasion of her privacy.

Right, he reprimanded himself, rolling his eyes skyward. *I'm condemning him, and I'm the one who stood outside her window and watched her undress!*

Still, he rationalized, what he'd done had been happenchance and harmless, even if it hadn't been right. What this guy was doing seemed deliberate and planned. His actions were covert as he continued his stealthy search of the desk drawers and moved on to her files. It was easy to see he didn't want what he was doing discovered.

All of a sudden Crew's mind was changed when it came to getting to know the young woman better. He was now feeling protective as well as randy. He owed it to her to find out what was going on.

Sure he'd taken advantage of her, watching her undress, but he'd meant her no harm. This guy, Crew wasn't so sure about. And until he was, he was going to dog the young woman's every move. He was going to insinuate himself into her life, one way or another.

By the time the young woman returned a few minutes later, the elegant young man had straightened any evidence of his hasty search and was sitting nonchalantly in a chair across the room awaiting her as though nothing untoward had gone on while she'd been gone.

As they left to go to the gym together, Crew finished the window and worked out a plan of approach.

THE FOLLOWING MORNING Alexia Grant was in a terrific mood as she sat outside on her patio lingering over a cup of coffee before she left for her office. Her happy disposition was due to Colby Langston's assurances that Gund & Associates was sure to take her on as a partner, especially if she landed the Funland Amusement Park account.

She had put in a lot of hours on the presentation and was happy with the way it was shaping up. But she wouldn't be satisfied until the proposal was as perfect as she could make it. Her attention to detail was the secret of her success so far. She left nothing to chance. Everything was planned. Alexia Grant was a control freak.

That control combined with sheer determination had gotten her from a background of poverty and hopelessness to a middle-class life-style. Only that was no longer enough. Having seen what life had to offer, she wanted the best. Her hard work and talent had made her an up-and-coming contender in the cut-throat world of advertising. She had sacrificed a lot, even a personal life, to get ahead, but the one thing she hadn't been willing to sacrifice was her principles. So it was taking her a little longer... but she was going to make it.

A pair of chirping robins caught her attention as they swooped and played in the sprinkler watering the lush grass in her large backyard. One of the sacrifices Alexia had made was being cooped up all day in a glass office tower. She tried to counter the long hours she spent at work with time spent cultivating the large flower bed in her backyard.

Butterflies and bees were regular visitors to the gay profusion of perennials in constant bloom. Her attention was drawn to the flower bed by a chubby chipmunk scurrying beneath a spray of moonbeams, his activity swaying the tiny yellow flowers. Alexia took a final sip of her coffee and rose to leave for her office.

Maybe if she got the partnership she would be able to put in the pondscape she'd been coveting since she'd seen it in a glossy edition of *HOME* magazine.

By the time she'd navigated the interstate to her office, her mind was far from the relaxing pleasures of gardening. As she punched her floor on the elevator, she was already visualizing the layout she had promised to have ready for a small chain of building supply stores. The ad didn't require much creativity, but the account was a steady, reliable source of income.

Her mind thus occupied, she didn't see Crew Harper lounging in the hall outside her office until she'd already collided with him.

"Oh dear! I'm terribly sorry, Mr. . . ?" Alexia said, stepping back hastily in embarrassment from the solid wall of his chest and looking up into his amused amber eyes.

"Crew," he answered, sticking out his hand.

Alexia switched her briefcase to her other hand and shook his offered hand, noting the calluses. "Well, ah...then...ah...Mr. Crew, if you'll excuse me please, I have work to do."

"No."

"Pardon?" Alexia said, stopping in midsearch for her key.

Crew grinned.

Oh, no, Alexia groaned inwardly. He was a flirt; he had a world-class flirter's grin. It was just too early in the morning for her to appreciate it, and she was very busy. Maybe if she humored him, massaged his ego for a moment, he'd go away.

"It's not Mr. Crew," the man informed her.

"It's not?"

Crew shook his head and leaned his shoulder against the wall.

"Then what *is* your name?" Alexia asked patiently.

"Harper's my last name," he answered, "but Crew will do. Crew's my first name."

"I see." Alexia nodded, wishing for another cup of coffee.

"What do you see?" Crew asked.

What she saw was a nonconformist, a handsome young man in pressed jeans, a navy shirt with a silver steer-head bolo tie slipped loosely around his neck and a western-cut jacket that hugged his wide shoulders. He was not terribly tall, maybe five-ten, and he was whipcord lean. Both his eyes and smile flashed, telling her that while he was nobody's idea of a yuppie, he was every woman's idea of a "real good time."

And she really didn't have time for him.

"How did you get past reception, Mr... ah...Harper?" she asked, abandoning the sparring match and trying to get on with it.

Crew shrugged. "I got here before they did."

"Is there something I can do for you?"

"As a matter of fact..."

Alexia's eyes shuttered. He wasn't going to go away easily. He wasn't going to go away at all. Subtle hints sailed past him like clipper ships.

"I did want to talk to you about something," Crew finished.

"You were waiting for me?" The truth finally dawned on Alexia.

"Sure. You don't think I lounge in strange hallways accosting women, do you?"

She didn't answer him, going instead in search of her key. Locating it, she opened the door to her office and ushered him in as she flipped on the light and got settled behind her desk, happy to have the barrier between them. Safer, too. Not from harm, from charm.

She could tell he was going to make a pest of himself, try to wear her down with his oodles of charm to get whatever it was he wanted. If she thought about it, and she wouldn't allow herself to think about it, his bad-boy attitude and lean arrogant body were sending out megawatt magnetism. If Crew Harper were anything, it was fun. And fun was something she hadn't allowed herself in a very long time. She'd been too busy for fun, directing all her waking hours to grabbing the brass ring.

All her attention had been focused on becoming a partner in Gund & Associates, the trendiest, yuppiest advertising firm in town. Because she didn't have the proper background, she'd had to work twice as hard as her more privileged competitors just to gain a foothold. Colby Langston, on the other hand, had breezed through the front door with nothing more than family connections.

"Okay," Alexia began, opening her appointment book and looking through it. "Perhaps we could set up a meeting later next week," she suggested.

"What for?" Crew asked, leaning back in the chair opposite her desk and crossing his arms in front of him.

"I thought you said you had some business you wanted to discuss with me. . . ."

"What's wrong with right now? I'm here, you're here . . ." He flashed that grin of his.

"I'm really very busy," Alexia pointed out, trying to stave off the admitted effect of his sexy grin.

Crew was having none of it. "Do you always schedule everything? Isn't there any room in your life for a bit of spontaneity? Don't tell me that little black book rules you. . . . Surely you sometimes act on impulse."

"I'm a professional," Alexia said icily.

Crew shrugged, unimpressed. "So am I."

"You haven't said exactly what it is you do. . . ." Alexia pointed out, besides turning women's knees to jelly, she thought to herself.

"I'm . . ." He couldn't tell her he washed windows without alerting her suspicions or risking her having seen him at some time and remembering. "Well, actually that's why I'm here to see you. I'm starting up my own landscaping business and I thought . . ."

She finished his sentence for him. "You thought I could work up a little something in the way of an advertising campaign for you, is that it?"

"Yeah, something like that."

"I'm very expensive," she said, trying to put him off.

"Really?" His eyebrows rose. "How expensive?"

Alexia's eyes narrowed as she considered him. Hadn't she seen him somewhere before? Something about him looked familiar to her. No, she decided, she'd have remembered him if she'd met him before. Crew Harper definitely made an impression on a woman. A hormone-zinging kind of impression. And it annoyed her that he did it so effortlessly.

Alexia leaned back in her leather chair, her elegant fingers toying with the thin silver hoops in her double pierced ear.

"I'm curious. What made you select me to bring your account to?" she asked, not really wanting to take on a new account because she was devoting most of her time to the Funland Amusement Park presentation. Still, she couldn't afford to turn down a client that had been recommended to her by another client. That sort of thing was bad policy, and she'd been in the game long enough to know protocol. She wasn't about to let a little slipup cause her professional suicide.

Crew rose from his chair and ambled over to the window. The drapes were still drawn except for the slight space he'd been able to see through the night before. He pushed the drapery to one side and looked down on the parking lot below, playing for time to come up with an answer she would buy.

He was glib, but she was intelligent. Her intelligence radiated off her with a sensual intensity. He knew his answer, though a lie, would have to be one she wanted to believe.

When he turned back to face her, he had his answer.

Reaching behind his neck to massage it with his hand, straining the buttons on his navy shirt in the process, he casually reported, "I overheard this guy at the gym telling this other guy that you were really good . . . that you knew your stuff and weren't just a pretty piece of fluff."

He threw up his hands, palms up, to ward off the criticism he saw was coming and winked. "Now don't go getting all sore at me. Those were his words not mine, sweetheart. Not that you're not pretty," he added, making her blush.

"You know this guy?" she asked suspiciously.

Crew shook his head and dropped into the chair he'd previously occupied. Crossing his ankle over his knee, he said, "No. I've seen him around. But you must know who he is, if he's recommending your work." Crew's eyes twinkled as he threw in the clincher, "He's a tall blond guy, who never goes near the weight room and looks like he has a butler to serve him his coddled egg and toast points on a silver platter for breakfast."

"Colby Langston," Alexia surmised, falling for his ruse of describing the guy who'd been riffling through her files yesterday evening when she'd left her office for a few moments. She smiled, pleased that Colby was an ally. It was a definite plus to have Colby and his monied connections in her corner, although Crew Harper didn't necessarily look monied. Maybe he was old money, the kind that was eccentric.

"Colby Langston a friend of yours?" Crew asked, studying her.

"We're sort of co-workers," Alexia said by way of explanation.

"Then you don't date?"

"Really, I don't think that's any of your concern," she said, the ice returning to her voice as she rested her elbows on her desk and steepled her fingers, planning to dismiss him. As Colby hadn't recommended her directly to the man sitting across from her, she was at liberty to dismiss him without violating any rules of protocol. Overhearing a conversation wasn't a recommendation, it was eavesdropping, and if Crew Harper eavesdropped, there was no telling what else he might stoop to doing.

He may have wormed his way into her office with his cocky, mischievous charm, but she definitely didn't need him complicating her life. Not now. Not when she was about to turn all her dreams into realities, if she were ever so careful.

Crew looked about as affected by her chastisement as a playful puppy. He was determined to get her to romp with him, as determined as she was not to, it seemed.

"I do apologize, Miss Grant. I was just wondering is all," Crew said, rising to his feet.

"Wondering what?" Alexia was amazed to hear herself asking.

Crew's grin was pure devilment. "Whether you scheduled your love life in that little black book as well."

"I think you should leave," Alexia said, annoyed and just a little amused in spite of herself.

"I'm about to," Crew said, slipping his long fingers into the front pockets of his jeans and rocking back on his heels with devastating masculine effect. "But before I go, I need you to answer one thing."

"What's that?" she asked, willing to concede an answer to whatever he wanted so he would leave her in peace, though she had a feeling he was going to disturb her long after he was gone.

"How expensive?" Crew asked, picking up the thread of their abandoned conversation.

"Oh, you mean . . . the advertising . . ." She grabbed a ludicrous figure from the air, one she was sure he wouldn't agree to. "One hundred dollars an hour," she advised him.

"One hundred dollars an hour!" he shouted.

"I'm very good."

"I don't doubt it—but one hundred dollars an hour! Do you know what some women will do for one hundred dollars an hour?"

"I work with my clothes on, Mr. Harper," she said coolly.

A mischievous look leaped into Crew's eyes. He was about to say something, then seemed to think better of it. Shaking his head, he said instead, "I don't think I can afford you, Miss Grant. A damned shame, too. I think we would work well together."

As he shook her hand, those calluses of his sending shivery thrills through her again, he grinned. "Maybe you'll change your mind."

"No, I'm quite certain," Alexia disagreed. "I'm sure however, that you'll be able to find someone more reasonable," she said with her warmest smile.

Reasonable didn't seem to be in his vocabulary. "Sure you couldn't just pencil me in that little black book of yours?"

"I'm sure."

Dear Editor:

Things are going pretty well, I think. There are a couple of teeny little things I may have forgotten to mention to you, however.

The hero, Crew, well you see, he's sort of a . . . Peeping Tom. But there are *these extenuating circumstances . . .*

As for the heroine, Alexia, it seems she has this little black book . . . in which she records everything.

Tiffany

2

ALEXIA GRANT SAT on her patio in the warm sunshine, once again enjoying her morning coffee before leaving for the office. The young man who had sought her out yesterday teased the corners of her mind as she watched a bluebird swoop down to splash in the stone birdbath at the edge of the garden.

Where had she seen Crew Harper before? Thinking back over their conversation in her office, she sought out some clue to his identity. Well, not identity exactly. She knew his name, but there was something about Crew Harper that disturbed her. No, besides *that*, she admonished her libido.

She snapped her fingers, startling the bluebird into flight, when she recalled Crew's mentioning he'd overheard Colby Langston recommending her to someone at the gym. That must be where she'd seen Crew Harper before...at the gym. He was certainly in great physical shape. Much better shape than Colby Langston in fact. Did that mean Crew used the weight room Colby avoided, she wondered.

Picking up her cup of coffee, she took a sip and stared unseeing at her flower garden. Her mind's eye was busy with Crew Harper. In a weaker moment she might have agreed to take on his account. Being in on the ground floor, helping to launch a new business could be fun. Who was she kidding—it was Crew Harper from the top of his head of dark wavy hair to the tip of his scuffed cowboy boots who could be fun. Remembering the megawatts of sexual chemistry and charm Crew Harper had radiated, she mentally changed the *could* to *would*.

Crew Harper was a Funland Amusement Park all by his little ol' self, she admitted to herself with womanly candor.

Glancing down at her chic designer watch she saw that she was running late and banished Crew Harper's lingering image from her thoughts. For the time being, all her attention had to be focused on gaining a partnership with Gund & Associates. She couldn't allow herself to indulge in sensual daydreams.

Still, before she left for the office, she took the time to snip some blossoms from the rose bed bordering the patio. Their gay colors and sweet fragrance always made her feel feminine and cherished. She wrapped them in a damp paper towel so they would hold fresh until she put them in a crystal vase of water on her desk.

Traffic was light, and she arrived at her building on time, despite her late start. Gathering her briefcase and the flowers, she headed inside.

"You shouldn't have . . ." a man's voice drawled with flirtatious amusement as she got off the elevator on the fourth floor and headed down the hall to her office.

It seemed Crew Harper's image didn't take too well to banishment. She'd managed to get him off her mind only to have him appear in the flesh, lounging outside her office door.

"But thanks just the same," he finished, taking the bouquet of pastel English tea roses from her and whisking them under his nose to inhale their sweet fragrance.

"They're not for you," Alexia said, shaking her head and rolling her eyes as she unlocked her office door to the sound of Crew's sneezing. She thought he was being amusing, but when she turned, she saw his eyes really were watering.

"You're a landscaper and you're allergic?" she asked. Before he could answer she went on to demand, "What are you doing here anyway?"

"Only to roses and everybody's got to be somewhere," he answered sequentially, flashing his playful grin.

"Fine, be somewhere else," Alexia said, arranging the tea roses in an art deco crystal vase on her desk, then emptying half of a large bottle of mineral water into the vase.

"But I like it here," Crew said, dropping into a chair and spreading his arms wide to encompass the room.

Alexia lowered her oversize glasses on the bridge of her aristocratic nose and glared at him. "Look, Mr. Harper—"

"Crew."

"Right. I'm really very busy, even if you're not. As you can see, I've got work to do," she said, sliding her glasses back in place and retrieving folders of paperwork from her zippered briefcase.

Opening a folder, she made a great pretense of studying its contents, but the print was a jumbled blur. She couldn't focus on the material with him watching her.

She would *not* look up. She was certain he would seize any sign of encouragement, so she forced herself to ignore him. Surely he would take the hint and go away.

"Ahem. . . ."

Alexia sighed, then looked up to his sunny smile and postured innocence.

She was having none of it. "Are you familiar with the word 'pest'?" she asked, closing the folder and folding her hands atop it with barely leashed exasperation.

"Careful, you'll hurt my feelings," Crew said, her censure sliding off him like satin sheets.

"Would that make you go away?" she asked hopefully.

Crew shook his head.

Alexia nodded. "I thought not. Tell me, Crew. What *would* make you go away?"

"That's easy," he said brightening. "You could agree to take on my account."

Alexia closed her eyes and rotated her fingertips on her temples. "I believe we already discussed this. I'm too expensive for you, remember?"

"Yeah, I remember," he said, rubbing his itchy nose with his knuckle. "But I got to thinking. . ."

His words were interrupted by the ring of the telephone on her desk.

"Oh, Hi, Colby," she said into the receiver. "Tomorrow night . . . ?" She glanced up to see Crew listening openly and rose and stood with her back to him to gain a measure of privacy. She rested her hip on the edge of her desk as she talked, comfortable in the taupe, double-breasted, softly tailored suit she wore. As she ended her conversation, she stretched like a cat, arching her back and raised her hand to massage her neck.

"I'll see you then," she said, ending her conversation with Colby and turning around to hang up the phone. "Now, you were saying . . ." she said, getting back to Crew who appeared to be lost in thought, a lazy sensual smile on his face.

"Earth calling . . ." she began, snapping her elegant fingers to gain his attention.

"Yeah, ah . . ." Crew answered, shaking his head to clear the image of her naked, imprinted there by her unconscious mannerism. His brow wrinkled. "I thought you weren't dating that Colby person."

"Whether or not I am is none of your concern, now is it?" she countered, slipping back into her chair.

Crew shrugged, no glib answer coming to him.

"About the reason you're here . . ." Alexia coaxed.

"Yes, well . . . I was thinking that perhaps you'd be willing to make some sort of deal."

"Deal?" Alexia repeated as if she hadn't heard him correctly.

Crew nodded.

"I don't think so. My fee is one hundred dollars an hour. I told you that yesterday. It's still true today."

Crew stretched out his lithe legs, crossing them at the ankles as he slouched in the flame-stitched chair opposite her desk. Folding his hands and resting them on his chest, he tapped his thumbs together and casually asked, "But isn't that a little steep?"

"It's my fee," she repeated, holding to the lie.

He nodded. Then like a persistent two-year-old he kept pushing. "But don't you ever make exceptions? I was thinking maybe you might in my case."

"Whatever gave you that idea?" Alexia asked, her eyes widening at his assumption.

Crew considered her a moment. "Umm...maybe you feel sorry for me?" he suggested, doing his level best to look pitiful, with basset hound eyes.

Alexia crossed her arms in front of her to stave off his admitted appeal. Leaning back in her chair, she said, "You don't strike me as the kind of man who needs my pity, frankly."

"I don't?"

Alexia shook her head.

With a resigned sigh, he abandoned his attempt to appeal to her motherly instincts as she obviously wasn't buying his little-boy appeal. Stretching his folded hands behind his head, he brought out the charmer, complete with killer grin, for her inspection. "Well, then how about because you like me?" he suggested, one of his amber eyes flashing a wink.

"Like you? *Like you!* I don't even know you. Now, if you'll please excuse me, I have work to do," Alexia said, trying to dismiss him before he talked her into something unwise. She felt herself becoming susceptible to a momentary flash of weakness.

"But you *could* get to know me," he said.

"I don't have time," she said, opening her black appointment book, this time the dismissal in her voice final.

Crew rose.

"You're a hard woman, Alexia Grant," he muttered, the amusement threading his voice making his observation sound as though he found her a challenge, one he intended to deal with nonetheless.

ALEXIA STARED AT THE WALL after he left. Crew Harper wasn't going to go away and leave her alone. She had a gut feeling about it. For some reason he was bound and determined to insinuate himself into her life. Sure, there was the man-woman thing; she'd have to be dead not to feel the electricity that crackled between them. But it was more than that. She was sure of it.

And unsure of what it could be.

What could Crew Harper know that she didn't?

CREW HARPER SAT in his truck in the parking lot looking up at the fourth floor of Alexia Grant's building. His eyes counted over and found the window of her office. The drapes were open.

He pictured her at her desk with sunlight spilling over her short tousled curls. Was she really working, he wondered, or was she merely impervious to his charm. He was 0 for 2 in his attempts to insinuate himself into her life.

There had to be a way. He just hadn't thought of it yet, he assured himself.

He'd have to manage it before the weekend was up because he started the windows of a new building on Monday. Besides that, Colby Langston was obviously continuing to try to use Alexia for whatever his secret purpose was. He'd like a chance at the high-rent pretty boy, just one shot.

But before he could find out what Colby was up to he had to wrangle a way to get close to Alexia. A way to spend time with her, so she would be relaxed enough around him to let down her guard.

"Think!" he muttered, beating his palms against the steering wheel of his truck.

His mind obeyed him...after a fashion. But the path his thoughts traveled was not intellectual. Crew imagined how Alexia had looked leaning over her desk, naked above the waist, her breasts sloping gently. His eyes were half-shuttered and his toes curled in his boots as he mentally reached out to touch her.

CREW MADE SURE he finished the windows on Alexia's office building early, allowing himself time to go home and change into pleated casual slacks and new deck shoes. To complete his "pass-for-yuppie" ensemble, he eschewed wearing socks when he slipped on the deck shoes and pulled on a T-shirt with a duck on it. No matter that the duck on the soft, worn cotton hugging his muscled chest and biceps was a cartoon figure.

He'd also tossed a battered gym bag containing a pair of gym shorts into his pickup, trying to cover all the angles. After all, he had no idea how Miss Alexia Grant spent her Friday evenings. He only knew he was determined to make himself a part of her Friday evening, fervently hoping it wasn't going to involve doing aerobics at some high-tech torture chamber. He'd already sweated enough up on the scaffolding and would much prefer somewhere that had comfortable chairs and air conditioning.

As the building emptied, he scanned the scattered groups of three and four, making sure Alexia didn't escape his notice. He had her car in sight, but it was possible she might leave with friends, riding along to a common destination for happy hour. Friday nights people tended to go out in groups, meeting people to date on Saturday night.

But Alexia wasn't in any of the groups calling out to one another across the parking lot as they made their way to trendy sports cars and European compacts. His was the only pickup truck in the lot. As the sun slipped lower in the sky, he wondered if he'd blown his watch and somehow missed her.

His fears were allayed a few minutes later when he saw her leave the building alone, carrying her briefcase and appointment book. He was relieved to see she still wore her classic double-breasted suit and hadn't changed into workout clothes. Maybe it was a sign the evening was going to go his way.

It had to. Crew Harper didn't bat 0 for 3. Not unless he was slipping.

Her gait was fluid and graceful as she strode to her white sports car. It was also full of confidence, Crew noted. He decided he liked that. The confidence made her sexy in his eyes—even sexier than the lush body under her somewhat tailored clothes that neither accented nor denied her femininity.

Alexia unlocked her car and tossed her briefcase and appointment book onto the back seat. As she slid behind the wheel, Crew unfolded the dark sunglasses he took from the sunvisor and put them on.

Alexia didn't know his pickup, and the sunglasses would conceal his identity if she happened to look in her rearview mirror and see him driving behind her. It would have been easy for him to walk up to her in the parking lot, but he wanted this meeting to look accidental. He did his best work thinking on his feet. Well, *some* of his best work thinking on his feet, he thought to himself, a wicked chuckle echoing in the cab of the pickup as he signaled a left turn and followed Alexia's sports car through rush-hour traffic until she reached her destination.... The parking lot of Cresswell's.

Considering the supermarket before him, he sighed. Well, he was getting air conditioning, even if he wasn't getting comfortable chairs. He gave Alexia a few minutes' head start, then followed her into the large store crowded with shoppers picking up their weekend groceries.

Circumventing the area where Alexia was, he moved several aisles ahead of her so she would think he'd arrived at the store before her when they ran into each other "accidentally." He remembered being out of dog food and picked up some on his way to the dairy section. There he staked out his wait with the fifty-pound sack of kibble balanced on his shoulder.

Sure enough, from the corner of his eye he saw her approach the dairy section. Busying himself with studying the milk case, he almost jumped at her, "excuse me," when she reached around him to select a container of coffee cream. Turning, Crew shifted the sack of dog food on his shoulder and the loose string cabling the end of the sack broke.

Hearing the commotion behind her, Alexia turned back from her cart, just catching Crew's soft curse. It wasn't until he pulled off his dark glasses that she recognized him and broke into laughter.

"You're working real hard on hurting my feelings, you know," he said, shoving his sunglasses on top of his head and dropping to his knee to begin scooping up the scattered bits of dry dog food on the floor.

Alexia surprised him by leaving her cart and joining him, kneeling to help him scoop up the mess he'd made.

"I take it you have a dog," she said, emptying a handful of kibble back into the sack.

"Yeah," Crew nodded, "only don't tell Sam. He doesn't think he's a dog. He thinks he's a cool dude."

"Cool dude, huh? Can't imagine where he picked up an attitude like that," Alexia taunted, picking up the last of the dog food while he held the sack open.

"At least he isn't a yuppie puppy," Crew shot back, hoisting the sack back onto his shoulder, one hand holding it closed as he followed her to the cart. Dumping the broken sack of food in her cart, he hitched his thumb and asked, "Mind if I grab a ride to the checkout lane?"

"Be my guest. We wouldn't want you to have your kibbles strewn all over Cresswell's now, would we."

"Ouch, that sounds downright painful," Crew mumbled, trailing her to the checkout lane.

"What are you doing for dinner?" he asked, keeping in step beside her.

"I'm eating in," she answered as they arrived at the checkout lane and she began putting her items on the conveyor.

"I could join you," he suggested.

"Aren't you forgetting Sam?" she asked, moving the cart after he lifted the broken sack from it to the conveyor.

"He's got food out. And I leave the TV on with the remote control on the couch so he can sit on it and change the channel every so often so he doesn't get bored."

"You're not serious..." Alexia said, lifting her grocery sack to leave as the checker began taping the broken dog food sack.

He was grinning and crossing his heart as she left.

"How much?" he asked the checker when she'd completed taping the broken sack.

"Oh, dear, I thought the two of you were together. The woman who just left paid for the dog food with her things."

Crew hurried from the store to try to catch Alexia only to get to his truck just in time to see Alexia pull out from her parking space. "Hey, wait up," he called, waving his hand, but she didn't see him, and her closed windows prevented her hearing him. Tossing the sack of dog food into the back of the truck, Crew got behind the wheel and sped after her.

Following his initial burst of speed, he slowed down, realizing he had a perfect excuse to follow her home. Once there, he could come up with a new proposition. She was bound to be more relaxed and susceptible to him on her home turf. Lulled by a false sense of security, who knew what the lovely Miss Alexia Grant might agree to, Crew thought, indulging a lusty daydream that drew heavily on the first time he'd seen her...

Ten minutes later he was so engrossed in the daydream he almost missed her turnoff. Swinging a hard right, he followed her to the end of a cul-de-sac. He honked when he pulled into her driveway behind her.

"What now?" Alexia asked, standing beside her car with her armload of groceries as she watched him amble toward her.

"The checker charged you for Sam's dog food," Crew explained, pulling out his wallet and offering her a twenty-dollar bill.

"Oh. Well, let me see how much it was. The receipt's in here," she replied, handing him the sack of groceries as she began digging in her briefcase that doubled as a purse.

"Don't you think we'd best get your cream and stuff inside out of the heat?" he suggested, starting up the walk toward the gray frame cottage with dark gray shutters and window boxes aspill with pink and white impatiens.

"Right. Okay, ah...just let me get the door," she said, zipping her briefcase and following him up the walk with her keys in hand.

The cottage was an open plan inside, and the kitchen was visible from the entrance. Crew headed directly there and placed the sack of groceries on the massive chopping block in the center of her all-white kitchen as Alexia continued her search for the grocery receipt. Remembering the half-and-half she'd selected from the dairy section, Crew set about putting away the perishables in her grocery sack.

When he opened her refrigerator, it yawned as empty as a school locker during summer vacation. "I take it you don't cook much."

"Not from scratch," she agreed.

"Then you must eat out a lot," he said over his shoulder.

"No, not really. I make use of the can opener and microwave. The only thing I make from scratch is chocolate cake . . . and love."

What? Nah, she hadn't really said that. Surely he'd imagined it. Or had the impulsive streak that had probably instigated the tiny butterfly tattoo on her tush just made an appearance? Holding his breath, he turned.

She handed him the grocery receipt, her face a mask of innocence. "Eight ninety-five and we're even," she said, holding her hand out, palm up.

"I've got a better idea," Crew countered.

Her eyes narrowed with suspicion.

"I could cook dinner for you...from scratch," he offered.

"Could you now..." Alexia studied him, her eyes contemplative. A hint of daring surfaced. "Okay, deal," she said, closing her wallet.

"Aw right!" Crew said, his hesitant offer replaced by enthusiastic anticipation. "Listen, since you're in a deal-making mood..."

"You're pushing your luck," she warned, setting her wallet on the counter.

"I only meant—"

"No."

Crew shrugged. "Okay, since you won't agree to making me a deal on the advertising for my landscaping company, how about we work out some sort of barter arrangement."

"Barter arrangement?"

"Yeah," he said, leaning back against the refrigerator and crossing his arms in front of him. His dancing eyes swept over her with masculine appreciation. "Isn't there *anything* I could do for you?" he drawled suggestively, flashing his killer grin.

She didn't blush as he'd thought she would. Instead she ignored his double entendre and repaid him with the same sensual survey of his body, hers daring to be even more leisurely than his. "Now that you mention it, there is," she finally agreed.

Hot damn! He hadn't imagined what she'd said.

"I'm listening," he said, all cocky charm.

Sidestepping the intimacy that had sprung up between them, she said, "Yes, now that you mention it, you could do something for me. You could not wear that ridiculous duck shirt again."

He made a mock stab at looking affronted. "But I thought all you yuppies loved ducks."

Alexia was barely able to suppress the amusement lifting the corners of her lips.

"No problem," he said with a friendly wink as he tucked his fingertips beneath the hem of the shirt and surprised her by whipping it up, cross-armed, over his head and off.

Alexia opened her mouth to object, but his next question stopped her.

"How about my pants, do you have any complaints about my pants?" he asked, hooking his thumbs in the waistband.

"No! No, they're fine," she croaked, unable to keep her eyes off the expanse of lean, sinewy flesh he'd exposed with such casual ease.

She watched him toe off the deck shoes he was wearing, freeing his bare feet, with an, "Ahh . . . much better."

He looked up to see her reconsidering her decision.

"I think you'd better go," she said, finding her voice.

"Why?"

"I have this rule . . . no shoes, no shirt, no service."

"You're kidding. . . ."

She shook her head. The yuppie was back, sentencing her impulsive nature to a back seat, while her practical, controlled side took over.

Instinctively knowing now was not the time to press her, Crew complied with her wishes. Reaching for his wallet, he extracted ten dollars and paid her for the sack of dog food before leaving.

THAT NIGHT they each lay in bed alone tossing restlessly as their thoughts mirrored each others', she wondering why on earth she'd ever made such a suggestive remark, cursing her tendency to act on impulse and he wondering if he'd actually heard her say it or had merely imagined it.

And both of them wondering what they would be like together... *making love from scratch.*

Dear Editor:

I do understand about heroes having certain standards to uphold. I promise to try to keep Crew in line.

And I was only kidding about Alexia's little black book. It's only an organizer to keep track of her business appointments.

Just because Alexia has a tattoo on her tush, you mustn't assume... Oh, dear, I did *mention the tattoo, didn't I?*

Tiffany

3

IT WAS AFTER nine when Crew opened his eyes the following morning. Sam, who'd been waiting patiently for his master to awaken, sat on the foot of the bed, his head between his paws and his tail thumping playfully. "'Morning, Sam," Crew said, rubbing the sleep from his eyes with the heels of his hands and yawning widely. Propping a pillow behind him, Crew sat up, reaching out to pet the dog. Sam rolled over at his touch, his tail swishing like a windshield wiper as Crew patted his soft, furry belly.

Crew groaned, knowing Sam was happily anticipating their daily morning run. After batting 0 for 3 with Alexia Grant, he'd spent the rest of the night downing long necks in a country and western bar. As a result his head throbbed and his mouth felt like an ash pit.

Reaching down beside his bed, he opened the bar-size refrigerator that served as a nightstand and withdrew a quart carton of orange juice.

When Crew had taken a couple of slugs, Sam began prancing on the bed, letting out a hopeful whine. The same kind of hopeful whine that had gotten to Crew when he'd found the mixed breed abandoned beside the road. Crew Harper was as soft on the inside as he was hard on the outside. It was something he went to great pains to disguise.

"Okay, pal, I'll run with you, but you have to promise to take it easy on me, okay," Crew said, throwing off the sheet and getting out of bed as naked as the day he'd been born.

Sam ran in excited circles around him, barking as Crew pulled on a T-shirt, some disreputable shorts and a pair of beat-up running shoes. After splashing cold water on his face, man and dog left the trailer on a slow run. As they ran Crew began talking.

"I met this girl, Sam . . ."

Sam barked.

"No, Sam, that's not the deal. You listen, I talk."

Sam whined once then settled into a quiet run.

"The thing is," Crew continued, "I don't know if I even like her. She's . . . well, she's a bit of a snob, actually. She's really pretty and probably plenty smart, but I'm guessing her values are real messed up. You see she's bought into this whole yuppie thing." Crew shook his head. "Still, she does have that tattoo on her tush..."

Sam whined again.

Crew fixed him with an eagle eye, "Shut up, Sam."

They reached the stop sign that marked the halfway point of their run and turned and headed back to the trailer. Sam's tongue was lolling sideways and the ash pit in Crew's mouth seemed to have caught fire. Sweat trickled down into his canvas shoes as he ran on the dusty path.

"The...ah...thing is...she needs...me," Crew said, his breathing becoming labored. A woman needing him was a very appealing prospect to Crew as he'd grown up reading comic books filled with adventure and dashing heroes who rescued heroines in peril. He still had the comic books; they had in fact grown into a valuable collection. But to his distress, he'd grown up with a generation of self-sufficient career women who didn't want or need anyone to fight their battles, leaving him a knight in shining armor who didn't quite know what to do.

Reaching the trailer, he plopped down on the grass. Colby Langston was the villain Alexia needed saving from, but how was he to tell her, he wondered. She'd never believe him if he came out and point-blank told her what he'd seen Langston do. Worse, she'd know he'd watched her undress. He could only help her by insinuating himself into her life. For a moment last night, when she'd let down her guard, he'd thought he'd succeeded. But he'd blown it by half undressing in front of her. He'd only been teasing her, but he'd gone too far, too fast and brought out her controlling side.

He couldn't believe he was 0 for 3. Maybe he *was* losing his touch.

"What do you think, Sam?" Crew asked when Sam trotted over and dropped his yellow tennis ball into his lap. "Am I losing my touch?" Sam's answer was to roll over on his back, wriggling and begging to have his belly rubbed.

Crew's laughter rang out in the quiet morning as he leaned forward to comply with the frisky mutt's begging. If only Alexia Grant had Sam's craving for attention. But she didn't. She'd made it quite clear to him that she didn't need anyone.

As he rubbed Sam's belly, Crew recalled the conversation he'd overheard Alexia having with Colby Langston on the phone in her office. They had a date for tonight. Rolling into a sitting position, Crew reached down and picked up Sam's raggy tennis ball, throwing it for him to fetch while he sorted out just what he was going to do about Alexia's date with Colby.

FIVE O'CLOCK found Crew parked in front of a van on Alexia's cul-de-sac, watching her house from the side-view mirror on his pickup truck. He was slouched in the driver's seat, his jacket and tie slung over the seat beside him. He'd brought them along just in case.

As he settled in to wait, he wondered what yuppies did for fun. Probably ate raw fish and shopped at office supply stores, he muttered to himself.

Two hours later he heard the purr of Colby's sleek European sports car as it crawled down the street like a cougar on the prowl. "Enemy at seven o'clock," he said, becoming alert.

Colby parked his car in her driveway and bounded up the walk to Alexia's door. Crew didn't think he'd ever bounded in his life. If he did, he hoped someone would shoot him and put him out of his misery.

Colby was dressed in khaki pants and a pink polo shirt, Crew observed, happy to see they weren't going anywhere that involved a tie.

When Alexia came out to join Colby, Crew saw she was wearing a lace-trimmed white blouse, jacquard vest and cognac-colored long skirt. The two of them together looked as though they had stepped out of some yuppie mail-order catalog and Crew wanted to gag. Where was the woman who'd had a tattoo put on her tush? Didn't she ever get to come out to play? he wondered, or had Alexia banished her to the background of her life while she pursued success at break-neck speed.

Colby helped Alexia into the car and backed out of her driveway, and Crew slouched even further in his seat as they drove by on their way out of the cul-de-sac. When Colby signaled a right turn, Crew started the pickup and began following them at a distance. Turning on the truck's radio, he switched the dial to a country and western station from the classical station Sam preferred to howl along with.

Colby's car pulled up in front of a building that was unfamiliar to Crew. It was understated in design and the sign outside gave no indication of what lay beyond the classic double wood doors. It simply said Wolff's.

Parking the pickup, he followed Alexia and Colby inside, keeping his distance.

The crowd inside had a patina of wealth. Couples spoke in well-bred whispers as they discussed the items that were up for sale, checking the elegant white catalogs describing each piece. Crew didn't need a catalog. It hadn't taken him more than a quick glance to see he was in an upscale gallery specializing in auctioning pieces from wealthy estates...and way out of his league.

The auctioneer was checking the microphone, and the crowd began disbursing to the rows of folding chairs set up in two sections with a wide center aisle. Crew watched as Colby placed his hand possessively in the center of Alexia's back and lead her up the aisle to seats near the front.

Out of curiosity, Crew went over and looked at the painting Colby and Alexia had been studying. To his eye it was ugly. The subject was a hunting dog with sad eyes who probably had a pedigree ten times better than his own. Turning from the painting, Crew took a seat across the aisle and about five rows behind Colby and Alexia.

"Well, hello there young man."

Crew turned to the elderly lady seated next to him. She was dressed entirely in lavender.

"Hello," Crew answered, trying not to stare at the small dog on her lap that was a matching shade of lavender. The dog was snoring softly, no doubt after a lunch of beef burgundy prepared by the lavender lady's chef.

"Can you tell me, young man, what do you think of number seventeen?" she asked as he tried to turn his attention back to Alexia and Colby, who had their heads close together.

"Number seventeen? Oh . . . I'm sorry. I don't seem to have my catalog. I must have set it down somewhere," Crew answered with a polite smile.

"The Chippendale chest with the carved wooden handles," she explained, pointing it out to him as the auctioneer began with an opening limit on the first item up for auction, a ten-inch enamel plate.

Noting the diamonds on each beringed finger of the lavender lady's pointing hand, Crew's mischievous nature asserted itself and he said, "You know, my dear, Mr. Michael and I were discussing that very piece for the shop. I don't think it would be very professional of me to give you an opinion on it. Why, dear lady, Mr. Michael would have my hide." Crew did his best effort at a convincing delicious shiver.

The woman beside him actually giggled. Then with girlish glee she said, "I simply must have it."

And have it she did a half hour later to the tune of $7,500.

Next up for bid was the painting of the hunting dog Colby and Alexia had been studying.

Colby made the opening bid, "Five hundred dollars."

Five hundred dollars! Crew mouthed silently in astonishment.

"Do I hear six?" the auctioneer called, anxious to get a bidding rally going.

A hand went up in the back row. Crew looked over his shoulder to see a smartly dressed man who could have been Mr. Michael had he actually existed.

"We have six hundred dollars, do I hear seven?" the auctioneer called out.

Colby's hand shot up.

"Seven to the gentleman up front in the third row. Do I hear eight?" The gentleman in back dropped out of the bidding. The auctioneer looked around anxiously, disappointed at having his rally cut off so quickly. "Anyone?"

Crew was amazed to see his own hand rise.

The auctioneer smiled broadly, smelling fresh blood. "We have eight," he sang out. "Do I hear nine?" he asked, looking to Colby.

Colby nodded.

"Nine! We have nine. A thousand...do I hear a thousand for this lovely painting?"

"One thousand," Crew heard himself saying as if in a dream.

Alexia turned and looked over her shoulder, her eyes searching out the person bidding against Colby for the painting. When her eyes met Crew's they widened... suspicion following swiftly on the heels of her initial surprise.

Crew winked, his broad grin confirming her suspicions that he was the one bidding against Colby.

Her eyes narrowed in censure as she whipped her head back around, the auctioneer rapturous as he continued his spiel, asking who'd give him eleven hundred.

Alexia whispered something to Colby, stilling the arm he'd been about to put up to signal eleven hundred dollars.

"One thousand once," the auctioneer said as his eyes swept the crowd sharply. "One thousand twice..."

"Oh, damn," Crew muttered.

The lavender lady giggled at his side. "So you like doggies, too, young man," she murmured. "Want to pet my precious Muffin?"

Crew gritted his teeth as she shoved her lavender dog into his hands and the auctioneer sang out "Sold to the man next to the lady in purple for one thousand dollars! Pay the cashier."

The lavender dog woke up and nipped Crew's hand. He quickly passed Muffin back to his owner, all the while thinking he couldn't even hang the ugly painting he was about to pay one thousand dollars for. Sam would take one look at the painting and bite him, too.

What had come over him? He didn't have one thousand dollars to throw away on impulse. His eyes narrowed. It was Alexia Grant's fault. Ever since he'd first laid eyes on her, he hadn't been able to think straight.

Making his way toward the cashier, he withdrew his checkbook. It was God's way of making him pay for his illicit peek at Alexia undressing. He accepted that. But one thousand dollars! With a shrug he admitted to himself it had been worth it.

After writing out the check and collecting his painting, he turned to see Alexia and Colby waiting at the back of the room near the door. Well, he certainly wasn't going to be able to follow them discreetly after this. Better to brazen it out.

"Oh, there...Miss Grant..." he called out in his best Mr. Michael's assistant voice.

Alexia turned as he approached.

"I thought I recognized you," Crew said, catching up to them.

There was nothing for Alexia to do, but to make introductions.

"Colby, this is Crew Harper. Mr. Harper, Colby Langston."

"Pleased to meet you," Crew said, extending his hand to Colby.

Colby nodded coolly, eyeing the painting Crew had clutched in his other hand.

"I rather had my heart set on that," Colby said, nodding toward the painting.

"What this? Really. Well since you're a friend of Alexia's I suppose I could sell it to you."

"You aren't especially fond of it?" Colby asked in surprise.

"Well, it's quite lovely, of course. But I don't have a personal attachment. Mr. Michael charged me with acquiring a hunting dog picture for a room he's doing. Another would do just as well, I'm sure."

"Alexia did say you might be willing to sell it to me for a profit," Colby said.

Crew glanced over at Alexia. "A profit...I see. Well, in that case, shall we say a hundred dollars over what I paid for the painting and it's yours."

"You're sure?" Colby asked, reaching for his checkbook.

"Quite," Crew answered, trying to avoid the daggers Alexia was shooting him over his charade as the fictitious Mr. Michael's assistant.

When the deal was completed, Colby magnanimously insisted Crew join the two of them for dinner as a token of his appreciation.

Crew looked back at Alexia. She was shaking her head no, her flashing eyes insisting he decline the invitation. It was perfectly obvious she thought the three of them having dinner together was anything but a good idea.

"Fine idea," Crew agreed, accepting and sending a covert wink Alexia's way.

Since Alexia looked as if she might act on impulse and go for his throat with her bare hands, Crew turned on the charm and kept the conversation rolling. "Where were the two of you planning on having dinner?" he asked.

"A sushi bar," Alexia invented, hoping to discourage him.

"Darn, I had sushi last night," Crew lied, giving Alexia back some of her own. "But tell you what, I know this place that has great steak. Why don't we go there, my treat since I just made a quick C note."

"That's sporting of you," Colby said, looking to Alexia. "Shall we?" he asked.

Crew's eyes dared her, calling her a coward if she declined his offer.

"If you like," she answered through gritted teeth, forcing a smile for Colby's sake.

"BUT THIS IS A HONKY-TONK!" Alexia said when they got out of their cars in the parking lot of Outlaws.

"Oh, you've been here before," Crew said smugly, trying to rile her barely leashed composure.

Alexia shot him a dirty look. She really was going to kill him, she decided, taking great delight in imagining slow and painful ways of doing it as they headed inside the rambling stone-and-timber building on the outskirts of town.

Crew requested a booth when they got inside and shortly found himself face-to-face with Alexia's simmering malice. The waitress came with menus and took their drink order. Alexia's eyes followed her to the long wooden bar jammed with rural and urban cowboys in new and old jeans.

There was something about a honky-tonk that got down to the bottom line of male-female real quick. She looked away from the sea of sexiness at the bar and into even more dangerous territory—Crew's amused amber eyes.

"Anything look good to you?" Crew asked.

"Excuse me?" Alexia choked.

Crew's smile was wicked as he nodded to the menu in her hand. "Colby and I have changed our minds about ordering steak. We've decided to order the barbecue ribs instead." Looking directly into her eyes he challenged, "Why don't you think about changing your mind...live a little. You never know, you might just like something different . . . something with some *bite*."

"Yeah, Alexia, why don't you try the ribs. It's the house specialty," Colby suggested, treading all over Crew's double meaning.

"Whatever," she agreed, closing her menu as the waitress returned to take their order, setting down two frosted mugs of icy beer and a glass of wine.

"Three rib specials," Crew ordered, "and another round of drinks when you bring the food."

"So, you're a decorator," Colby said, looking at Crew a little doubtfully.

"No . . . Oh, you mean Mr. Michael." Crew thought fast. "Ah . . . you see I do a favor here and there for him and he sends the occasional client my way." Crew chugged a couple of undecorator-like swallows of cold beer to dispel any doubt.

"Then what is it that you do exactly?" Colby asked, wiping at the wet ring his icy mug was leaving on the table.

"I dig up dirt."

Colby looked a little pale.

"He's in landscaping," Alexia explained with a pained expression.

"I see," Colby nodded, looking considerably more relaxed.

"How about you?" Crew asked.

"Advertising."

"The two of you competitors?" Crew asked, taking a swallow of beer.

"We both work at Gund & Associates," Colby said, not really answering Crew's question.

"No kidding? I've been trying to get Alexia here to work me a deal on some advertising for my company. You wouldn't happen to be a partner who could influence her to look favorably on my proposal, would you?"

Colby laughed. "Hardly. I'm not ambitious, to my father's eternal dismay. I'm just killing time until my trust fund kicks in."

Crew turned his attention back to Alexia. "How about you, you got one of those trust fund things, too?"

Alexia shook her head. "No trust fund. I'm the one working on being a partner," she admitted, playing with the stem of her glass.

The waitress returned with their dinner order, setting down the three rib platters piled high with golden fries and slaw.

Conversation waned as they began enjoying the tempting meal. When they finished, coffee was ordered while the band began tuning up for the evening. Before long couples congregated on the wooden dance floor, the lyrics of Bob Seeger bouncing off the walls.

They were halfway through their coffee when the first ballad began. Crew glanced over at Colby. "Mind if Alexia and I dance to this one?"

Colby didn't have the right to mind, but Alexia was hoping he'd object. His casual shrug infuriated her.

Crew got to his feet and stood beside the booth, offering her his hand. She wanted to refuse, but she knew if she did, Crew would give her a hard time. So she gave in to the inevitable and allowed him to lead her onto the dance floor.

Honky-tonk dancing was intimate. Everyone on the dance floor was dancing close . . . women's hands on men's shoulders and men's hands on women's waists. The crush of the crowd created an anonymity and a sort of group sensuality. To dance otherwise would be obvious, and one thing Alexia did not want to do was give Crew Harper any reason to hassle her. He was better at hassling than any five men she knew.

So she didn't object when he pulled her to his solid chest, fitting her head just under his chin. He smelled of soap and hickory smoke, but all she smelled was a rat. And when he settled his hands just a tad south of her waist, she repeated her mental vow to kill him.

The male singer was crooning lyrics that were as suggestive as the slight pressure of Crew's hands on her hips as he urged her closer.

"I agreed to dance with you, not have your children," Alexia snapped.

"Ah, but they'd be beautiful children, wouldn't they?" Crew whispered, unfazed by her censure.

"Don't you have somewhere else to be?"

Crew chuckled, his breath warm and sexy near her ear. "Tell you what, give me one really good dance and I'll leave."

"Promise?"

"Scout's honor," he agreed, raising his hand, palm forward.

"Give me a break, *you* were never a Boy Scout."

"Sure was. You should see my badges sometime."

"Does that approach work for you a lot?"

"Why won't you believe I'm a nice guy?"

"Nice guys don't bargain for one really good dance, that's why."

"About that dance..." he said, his grin lazy and wicked as the band broke into a sexy, saxy version of "Closer to You."

"You'll leave then... promise?" Alexia hedged.

Crew nodded.

Maneuvering Crew deeper into the crowd and out of Colby's line of vision, Alexia painted her body against Crew's and planted a hot, wet seductive kiss on his lips, taking advantage of his openmouthed astonishment. Much like the tattoo she'd gotten, the kiss was over quickly, but definitely felt and left an indelible mark. The song ended.

It seemed the same girl who'd gotten a tattoo gave out impulsive kisses and it didn't take Crew Harper more than a heartbeat to realize he liked this side of Alexia Grant one hell of a lot.

Smiling with mischief, Alexia looked up at him, winked and whispered familiar words back at him, "You're a hard man, Crew Harper."

All he could manage to say was, "Walk in front of me," as he followed her back to the table.

Alexia slid into the booth next to Colby as Crew picked up his jacket and the tab.

"I have to be going," Crew said, taking his leave in a bit of a hurry.

"Thanks for selling me the painting," Colby said, waving him off.

"Is there anything wrong?" Colby asked, turning back to Alexia.

"No, . . . why?"

"Nothing," Colby said with a shrug. "You just look kinda funny."

Look funny. . . she *felt* funny. She hadn't figured on Crew kissing her back.

She smiled weakly at Colby. He was the kind of man she had planned for her future. So why did Crew Harper make her so hot?

Dear Editor:

Yes, Alexia's tattoo is in good taste, so not to worry. It's only a little butterfly symbolizing her free spirit.

Did I say free spirit? Well I must have been mistaken. All Crew did was take off his shirt and Alexia threw him out. How, I ask you, am I going to conduct a proper romance if she quails at the sight of a man's bare chest?

Tiffany

4

"TRUCE," CREW PLEADED, holding up a white sack when Alexia answered her front door the following morning.

"Go away," she said, embarrassed by her disheveled state when she saw who her early-morning caller was.

"Aw, come on, Alexia, you wouldn't want to be the one to break my perfect record, now would you?" he asked, a teasing twinkle in his eyes.

"Your perfect record?" She tugged at the neck of her robe.

"No woman has ever refused to join me in the sack," he said, wriggling his eyebrows lasciviously and shaking the white bakery sack in his hand.

Alexia meant to discourage him but instead found his playful mood catching. He was either a tonic to the workaholic life-style she'd adopted since joining Gund & Associates . . . or a bad influence, more likely the latter.

"Make me want to join you in the sack," she said, crossing her arms in front of her, defensive in her dare.

He leaned in close, waving the fragrant bakery sack beneath her uppity nose. "Flaky, buttery croissants, still warm from the oven . . ." he said, his breath near her ear sending delicious shivers down her spine that had nothing to do with a hunger for food.

She looked at him as if he were both poison and antidote.

"Did I mention they were filled with chocolate?" Crew coaxed, his tongue poking the inside of his cheek.

"No fair. That's taking unfair advantage," she accused, stepping back to let him inside.

"Oh, and you don't?"

"What do you mean?" she asked, pulling the sash on her robe tighter.

"Kissing me senseless on the dance floor last night for example," he answered.

"You deserved that."

"Yeah, I guess I kinda did," he agreed, his wide sexy grin making an appearance. It hadn't sounded like an apology.

"It didn't mean anything," she was quick to explain. "I just did it on impulse to get your goat."

"My goat . . ."

"You know what I mean."

"Yeah, I think I do. But I didn't think you ever acted on impulse. I thought everything you did was carefully planned and duly noted in that little black notebook of yours."

"You're right. I do try not to act on impulse. I think it's the wisest course."

"Anyone ever tell you maybe you think too much? You ought to take a chance on going with your feelings sometimes. You might be surprised."

Alexia had a feeling he was the one who'd be surprised if she went with her feelings of the moment and jumped on him. It wasn't fair that a man could roll out of bed, run his hand through his hair, splash water on his face and throw on jeans and a T-shirt and look as heart-stoppingly handsome as he did. The very air around them crackled with erotic possibilities.

Playing safe, she said, "Well, right now I feel like having some coffee with cream to go with your croissants. Why don't you make a pot while I get dressed?"

He had a white dish towel tossed over his wide shoulder when she returned to the kitchen five minutes later. Her nose was assaulted by the spicy aroma of cinnamon coffee brewing in the automatic coffee maker on the counter. Her stomach grumbled as she anticipated the treat Crew had brought.

"Oh, you're back," Crew said, glancing over his shoulder to see she'd changed into what looked like a big scarf. She'd somehow twisted the big print square of silk chiffon into a calf-length dress with a halter top and a sarong tie at her hip. Though the bright square of material covered her lush body, it hugged her curves like a race car.

"Let's eat out on the patio, since it's such a pretty morning," she suggested.

"Sure. How about some music?" he asked, pouring them both a cup of coffee with cream.

"What kind of music do you like?" she asked, walking over to the stereo system as he put the croissants and coffee on a tray to carry them outside.

"Anything with a saxophone in it is fine," he replied, hoping to infuse some romance into the atmosphere she seemed bent on keeping merely cordial.

A sardonic smile tilted his lips when he heard the music she'd selected. His hope for a more romantic atmosphere hadn't exactly been met. Bruce Springsteen was belting out "Born in the U.S.A." on the stereo housed in her pine armoire next to the fireplace. There was a saxophone in the band, true. But it was more rowdy than sensual...nothing like the sultry saxophone solo Crew remembered playing in his head when he'd watched her undress in her office or the one backing up the lyrics to "Closer to You," the love song from *The Big Easy* the band had been playing when she'd laid that surprise kiss on him.

Alexia seemed to be sending him a whole array of signals, none of them very clear. Or perhaps he didn't want to get the message she was sending him. After all, despite his sexy daydreaming, she'd only invited him to share breakfast, nothing more. Just because a woman wore something he found provocative didn't give him a license to assume. And even the breakfast idea had been his, not hers, he had to remind himself.

Still, he did have a decided edge on seduction. While it was an advantage he'd gleaned unfairly, it was an advantage nonetheless.

He knew about her. Knew about her secret butterfly tattoo. Knew about her inclination to give in to the occasional impulse.

His conscience rode him hard as he picked up the tray and followed her out to the patio. On the way he silenced his conscience with the rationalization that he was seducing her for her own good. He had to get close to her to find out what Colby Langston was up to.

When he stepped outside, he wasn't prepared for the pocket of loveliness that greeted them. The view from Alexia's patio was a delightful surprise. While he had expected the rosebushes that ringed her patio, he hadn't expected the carefully tended flower garden that was in full bloom, the riotous colors of the zinnias and marigolds. He appreciated the view, but he also knew the amount of hard work involved in tending such a large flower garden.

The idea he'd conceived earlier now had a focus. The roses in Alexia's office had told him she most probably lived in a house instead of an apartment. Houses had yards that needed maintenance and landscaping. He could barter his services for hers.

Setting the tray down on the umbrella table, he said, "About this barter arrangement we agreed to . . ."

"We agreed to . . . I didn't agree to any such thing and you know it."

"But you do have to agree it's the perfect solution to our problem."

"*You* have a problem. *I* don't."

"Sure you do, Alexia," he assured her with his wicked grin. "*I'm* your problem."

Alexia took a sip of her coffee and then set it down on the bistro table with a resigned sigh. She knew determination when she saw it. It was her own strong suit after all. "What exactly did you have in mind?" she asked, lifting a still-warm croissant to her lips.

"I like an intelligent woman," Crew said, "one who knows when she's beaten."

"Oh, I'm not beaten. I just know when to pick my battles, and this one isn't a priority at the moment. I have a bigger battle to win."

"There you go hurting my feelings again," Crew said, not looking the least bit wounded.

"Right. Now what was it you had in mind?" she asked, bringing the subject of the barter back on the table as she licked the chocolate from inside the croissant.

"Ah-choo! Well, first I think we should tear out all these damn rosebushes," he said, rubbing his itchy nose.

"I like roses," she stated adamantly.

"But don't you feel sorry for me?" he pleaded, thwarting another sneeze.

"I believe we've already established that I don't."

"You're a hard woman, Alexia Grant," he muttered making his way through the rosebushes to the yard. Walking over to the side of the yard where the large flower garden was planted, he saw Alexia had an eye for color and design. The taller flowers like irises were planted as background and ground cover edged the smooth gray stone border.

He rubbed his itchy nose again, then made what he considered a generous offer. "Suppose I tend the garden, mow the lawn and prune your trees for the rest of the season in exchange for your working up an advertising layout for me to use to start up my landscaping business."

"I like tending the garden. It relaxes me. And I have a service that does the lawn stuff."

She was purposely being difficult, he decided, returning to the patio.

"How about your garden?" he suggested. "I could expand it for you so you could have a cutting garden from early spring to late fall."

"I don't think so. The size it is now is about all I can handle."

A pair of butterflies began playing tag in the flower garden as he sipped his coffee trying to come up with something she'd agree to barter her services for. "You know it really is lovely back here, restful . . . peaceful."

"I know. Sitting out here helps get rid of the stress and tension of my job. I've been thinking of putting in a fish pond with some water lilies and cattails. I just saw one in a magazine but I'm sure it would be too expensive to even contemplate. Besides, I don't have time right now to think about tackling such a project with the work I have scheduled at the office."

"But that's it!" Crew exclaimed, snapping his fingers. "I could build the fish pond for you. You wouldn't have to worry about a thing."

"What?"

"The barter arrangement," Crew explained. "I could be building the fish pond you want in exchange for your advertising services. It's a perfect barter arrangement—your expertise for my expertise."

"Are you sure?" Alexia asked, looking at him skeptically, not for a single minute believing his claim that she could trust him. Men like Crew Harper put a spin on the word trust. Trust for them was an adjustable concept they fitted to the occasion or personal need of the moment.

"Sure, I'm sure," he answered, not really sure at all.

He didn't have a clue about how to build a fish pond, or even exactly what one was. But how hard could it be? Besides, she'd said she'd seen a picture in a magazine of exactly what she wanted. All he had to do was look at the picture, use it for a plan and do some research on the actual construction that would be required.

"You said something about having a magazine with a picture of the kind of fish pond you want . . ." he said, waiting for her to bite the hook he'd baited.

"Yes, it's inside. I'll go and get it for you to take a look at. Once you see what I'm talking about, you might want to change your mind about doing it. I'll just be a minute. Do you want some more coffee?" she asked.

He shook his head and watched her sexy form disappear through the door. No way was he going to change his mind. Building a fish pond in her backyard was a perfect setup. She wouldn't be able to ignore him when he was constantly underfoot.

Crew finished the last bite of croissant and pushed the plate aside. Rubbing his hands together, he said to the garden at large, "Colby Langston, meet Crew Harper, detective extraordinaire."

"Here's what I was talking about," Alexia said, returning to the patio and setting the open magazine before him.

Crew glanced down at the picture and back up at Alexia. "Like I said, no problem."

"When do you think you could start?" she asked, taking a seat across the table from him when he looked as though he was going to pull her down into his lap.

"I can come over tomorrow around noon to begin taking measurements and laying out a plan. Meanwhile, why don't you be thinking about exactly how big you want this fish pond to be."

"How long will it take you to finish the job?" she asked, beginning to wonder about the wisdom of agreeing to this barter arrangement of his. He was going to be underfoot for a good deal of time. But at least he'd be there during the day when she was at work. If she worked late, as she often did, she could arrange not to have to see that much of him. Even though she wanted to, she thought, looking at his head bent over the magazine. Crew Harper was fun to look at. Fun to be with. Fun.

"Now we come to the fine print in the contract," Crew said, leaning back in his chair.

"I should have known," Alexia said, a frown of disappointment pulling at her mouth.

"No, now wait. It's nothing you can't live with."

"I'll be the judge of that," she said, folding her arms across her chest.

"Okay, okay," he said, throwing up his hands, palms up. "Here's the deal. Until I get the landscaping business set up, I need to continue my regular job. That means I can only work on your fish pond evenings and weekends."

"Oh, no, that won't do at all," she began objecting, knowing her own strengths and weaknesses where men were concerned. Crew Harper was beginning to head the weaknesses column, and getting a partnership at Gund & Associates didn't allow that particular indulgence.

"I promise I'll be good. You won't even know I'm here," he said, "Scout's honor."

She did want the fish pond. And if she stayed inside working on the Funland Amusement Park account, she'd be able to avoid spending any amount of time with him.

"I know I'm going to regret this, but okay... deal," she agreed, sticking out her hand.

He took it, but with both his hands sheltering hers. "Why don't you have dinner with me tomorrow night to seal the deal."

"I've ah... got plans."

"You're not going out with Buttercup again tomorrow night, are you?"

"Buttercup?"

"Yeah, you know. That plastic boy-doll you were with last night," Crew said with a smirk.

"His name is Colby Langston."

"Whatever..."

"And who I go out with is no concern of yours. Our agreement is strictly business."

"Right."

THAT EVENING Crew lay in bed studying the book he'd gotten from the local library on building a fish pond. It looked easy enough. He'd have to dig a large hole, then put down newspapers that would deteriorate in time into a paste beneath the special plastic tetra liner he laid over them. After anchoring the liner with large decorative rocks around the edge, all he had to do was landscape, stabilize the water and add fish.

He closed the book and grinned big time. *A piece of cake.*

ON MONDAY EVENING Crew and Alexia came to terms on the layout and size of the fish pond he was to construct for her as his part of their barter agreement, even if they hadn't come to terms with the very real attraction between them.

At seven Colby Langston had arrived to escort Alexia to a meeting of the Regional Commerce and Growth Association where he could introduce her to the movers and shakers in the community he had family connections to . . . potential clients.

Crew didn't have a family, much less family connections. His father had worked himself into an early grave as a coal miner and his stepfather had made it clear straight off that he didn't want him around. As soon as he'd graduated from high school, he'd left town. He'd taken any job he could find to survive. Any job that was outdoors. He couldn't stand being cooped up as his father had been.

Working hard, he'd saved his money and wanted to start his own business. Not because he was particularly ambitious but because he wanted to be independent. His father's early death had taught him not to count on anyone but himself. Sam was about as much of a commitment as he intended to make.

Sam was with him Tuesday night when Alexia arrived home from her office.

"She's home," Crew said when Sam stood and pricked up his ears. "She's the dishy dame I've been telling you about. You remember, the one with her nose stuck in the air and a secret tattoo on her tush. Let me know what you think when she comes out to meet you, boy."

Crew's shirt was hanging on a limb of a nearby tree and his jeans were damp from the exertion of digging in the rocky ground. He hitched them up from where they were riding low on his hips and wiped the back of his wrist across his sweaty brow.

Leaning on the shovel he was using to dig the fish pond, he waited and watched. Sam waited and watched at his side.

They both waited in vain. When it was patently apparent she wasn't coming outside, Crew swore and began digging again.

Sam laid back down, resting his head between his paws. His big brown eyes looked up reproachfully at Crew and then he barked.

"Shut up, Sam."

ALEXIA STOOD at the kitchen window and watched as Crew and his dog drove away in Crew's rusty old excuse for a truck.

It had taken all her willpower not to go out and greet him when she'd gotten home. She'd told herself it was because she had work to do on the Funland Amusement Park account. While that was true, it wasn't the uppermost reason. The *real* reason was, that bare chested and sweaty, Crew had looked gorgeously virile and way too inviting. And what he was inviting was down-and-dirty fun. It was glittering in his eyes every time he looked at her.

Why did he stir up such lascivious daydreams... and why didn't Colby?

And Crew had looked strangely familiar again. Where had she seen him before?

THE FOLLOWING EVENING Crew was determined not to be ignored so easily. When Alexia arrived home from the office he and Sam were sitting on her front porch waiting for her.

Seeing them, Alexia sighed, then gathered her things from the seat beside her. She approached the two of them intending nothing more than a curt hello.

"This is Sam," Crew said when she drew near.

"What happened, was there nothing good on television for him to watch?" she asked, searching her bag for her key.

"No. As a matter of fact, Sam gave up a Lassie rerun so he could meet you."

Alexia looked dubious.

"Okay, actually I thought since Sam's alone all day, I'd bring him along when I work on the pond."

"As long as he doesn't dig up my rosebushes," Alexia said, unlocking the door.

"I'm the one more likely to do that," Crew muttered, casually strolling into the house after her with Sam close on his heels.

"What's that?" she asked, not quite hearing as she reached the kitchen ahead of him.

"Nothing."

"Want some lemonade?" she offered, taking a pitcher from the refrigerator. "I think the humidity must be over a hundred today. I thought I was going to melt when I got into my car."

She poured them both a glass of lemonade and a bowl of water for Sam. "You aren't planning on working in this heat?"

He shook his head. "I thought maybe I'd take you for a ride."

Alexia was thinking that would be redundant when he began explaining. "No, really. There's a park about a ten-minute ride from here called Lone Elk Park. I noticed some ferns growing wild and I thought you might want to cultivate some around your pond. If you like them, I'll see if I can locate a source."

"I see."

"Then you'll go?"

"As soon as I change," she agreed.

"There's no need for that. We'll only be gone a short while."

She capitulated and followed him back outside to his battered old truck. "Wouldn't you rather take my car?" she asked, eyeing his truck with obvious trepidation.

"I would, but you wouldn't. Sam sheds."

"Oh."

With a resigned sigh, she tackled the task of climbing into the truck, no easy feat in high heels and a slim, tailored suit.

Crew merely grinned when she had to slide her skirt high on her thighs to accomplish the step up. His hand fleetingly touched her bottom, giving her the added leverage to assist her climb into the high bench seat of the truck.

When she was settled, Sam began to bark.

"Mind sliding over a little?" Crew asked.

When she made no move to do as he suggested, he explained, "Sam's used to riding shotgun by the window. He likes his ears to fly in the wind, I guess."

Sam whined at her feet and began wagging his tail as he cocked his head and looked up at her expectantly.

"I bet I know who trained you to like it, too," she muttered, sliding over so that Sam could hop up into the truck beside her.

When Sam was in place, Crew popped open the glove box and withdrew a plastic bottle.

"What's that?" Alexia asked.

"Transmission fluid," he answered. "The transmission's been kinda temperamental lately so I feed it regularly."

"Oh," Alexia commented, looking rather sick.

"Don't worry. It hasn't broken down on me yet."

"It's the 'yet' part of the statement I don't find reassuring," Alexia sassed.

"Boy, you sure are a pessimist," Crew said with a shake of his head as he closed the door of the truck and opened the hood to add transmission fluid.

Alexia was thinking that now would be a good time to tell him she'd changed her mind, when he closed the hood and came around to the driver's side. Somehow she lost her voice when he climbed up beside her, his thigh pressing warmly against hers.

She would have moved over, but at that moment, she noticed Sam's incisors were the size of small mountains. He seemed to be grinning at her while he panted.

"Does your dog ever bite?" she asked, eyeing Sam with hesitant speculation.

"Not unless I tell him to. Just be real nice to me and you'll be perfectly safe."

"Yeah right. From Sam."

Crew's wicked grin looked even more lethal than Sam's, even if his teeth weren't showing. And Alexia was sure Crew's bite was at least as bad as his bark.

The truck sputtered and popped as they pulled out of her driveway, with the background accompaniment of Hank Williams Junior on the radio.

When they were on the road, Sam began scratching at the radio with his paw.

"What does he want?" Alexia asked.

"The second button on the left," Crew explained. "Mind pushing it or he'll never give us any peace."

Alexia reached out and pushed in the button on the radio. The truck was instantly flooded with classical music. Sam sat back contentedly, cocking his head to listen, grinning again and showing his incisors.

"Sam likes classical music?" Alexia asked in disbelief.

"Yeah, it's weird. I have to listen to the stuff whenever Sam comes riding in the truck. I made the dumb mistake of teaching him to howl along with it one day as a joke."

As if on cue, Sam began his howling accompaniment to the music.

Alexia didn't know whether to laugh or cry as she rode along in the lurching, sputtering truck sitting between a singing dog and the sexiest man she'd ever met. What she did was slide down in her seat, praying no one would see her.

"It says no dogs allowed in the park," Alexia said hopefully, reading the sign posted at the entrance to Lone Elk Park when they reached it a short time later.

"So it does. But Sam's cool. He'll be in the truck with us. The rangers post the sign so dogs aren't let free to run around terrorizing the wild animals that live in the park."

"Oh." Alexia slunk a little further down in the seat. She didn't like disobeying rules.

"You'll never see anything if you don't sit up," Crew admonished her.

"I can see."

"Maybe . . . but what are people going to think when they see the truck go by and just the top of your head barely visible," he teased.

She bolted upright to the accompaniment of his laughter.

"That's much better," he said, sliding his arm across the back of the seat and driving at a leisurely crawl through the winding park roads.

"Oh, look," she said as a flock of birds lifted off the lake that was the scenic centerpiece of the park.

"Yeah, they sure are pretty, aren't they. Next time we come we can bring along some stale bread to feed them."

Next time? Alexia thought. His conversation was beginning to imply an ongoing relationship. Maybe she should nail him down on just how long this project was going to take. Her thoughts were distracted when he pulled up to the stock gate and stopped the truck.

"Sam, you wait for us in the truck. Okay, boy?" Crew said, climbing down from the truck and helping Alexia down beside him. "Take my hand and I'll help you across the stock gate," he said.

"But the sign says to stay in your vehicle once you cross the gate," Alexia objected, not taking his offered hand.

Crew raised his hands to his hips. "You're one hell of a reader, aren't you?"

She didn't deem to answer him, just held her ground.

"Do you *always* do everything you're supposed to?" he asked.

"Don't you?"

His grin was sufficient answer that of course he didn't.

"They have a perfectly good reason for their rules, I'm sure," she continued to object.

"Oh, for heaven's sake. I'm only going to break it a little bit. The ferns I want to show you are just over the fence by the little winding stream there. Look around, you don't see any buffalo ready to charge, do you?"

"No," she agreed, after checking *very* carefully.

"Okay then, we'll take a quick look and get back in the truck and drive on through like good law-abiding citizens."

"Do you promise?"

"Promise. I'll have you back home safe in an hour, and you can tell Buttercup all about your wild adventure."

Alexia could see she wasn't going to be home anytime soon unless she agreed to go look at the ferns. "Okay," she said, giving him her hand and following after him, her eyes peeled for a stampeding herd of anything. It was kind of difficult as she also had her eyes peeled for anything that crawled or moved on the ground at her feet.

When they reached the stream, she saw the ferns he'd been speaking of growing in masses along the bank.

"What do you think?" he asked. "Would you like some of these framing your fish pond?"

"You're not going to steal them, are you?"

"I've never stolen anything in my life," he said, looking highly affronted.

Maybe, Alexia thought. But only if you didn't count the hearts he'd been stealing since the day he'd been born.

"Okay, now that I know you like the ferns, we can go. I'll see what I can do about locating a legitimate source."

When they reached the truck, Crew gave Alexia a big grin and said, "You did that real good."

"What?"

"Pretending not to notice that big ol' buffalo mosey-ing down the side of the hill toward us."

"What buffalo?" She turned and looked over her shoulder, and sure enough, he'd been telling the truth. She hopped into the truck and slammed the door closed, taking over Sam's shotgun seat at the window.

Crew took his time ambling around to the driver's seat. He was still chuckling when he climbed in beside Sam and started the truck.

"I'm glad you think it's funny. We could have been killed!" she fumed.

"I would never let anything happen to you. I'm a former Boy Scout, remember?"

The look she gave him told him she wasn't im-pressed. "Do you think you could put this thing into gear and scout our way out of here?" she said, lifting her hair off the back of her neck. "And while you're at it, turn up the air conditioning. I'm melting."

"Yes, ma'am."

The truck sputtered and lurched as it crossed the stock gate and slowly began its chugging ascent up the hill. The buffalo eyed them curiously but didn't at-tempt to follow, Alexia noted to her relief.

When they reached the top of the highest hill, sev-eral head of moose with huge antlers moved away from the barbecue pits they were rummaging in and began ambling toward their truck looking for handouts.

Did the truck seem to be slowing down or was it her imagination? Alexia wondered as the animals ap-proached the truck.

"Uh oh . . ." Crew said, glancing over at her, shamefaced.

"You *aren't* going to tell me you've run out of gas . . ."

"No, but I think the transmission just went. I can't get the truck to do anything more than coast."

Looking down, Alexia saw that Crew was pushing the gas pedal all the way to the floor and the truck was only inching along.

"What are we going to do?"

"Try to coast out of the park. The rest of the way is mostly downhill. I don't have a leash in the truck for Sam so we can't get out while we're still in the park."

"Don't worry," Alexia said, eyeing the moose looming over the car. "I wasn't planning on it."

She held her breath as the truck slowly rolled down the winding path, gathering speed as it went.

"Tell me you have brakes...ple-ease..." Alexia said, her feet pressing against the floorboard instinctively as if she could help control the truck's speed.

"Oh, we've got brakes," Crew answered. "But I want to use them sparingly so we can gather enough speed to take us on out of the park when we hit the flat ground."

The truck coasted out of the park and onto the service road. A hundred or so yards onto it, the truck came to a complete stop, despite Alexia's whispered coaxing.

"Now what?"

"I'm going to try to add some transmission fluid. Maybe it's only a seal."

A few minutes later Alexia heard Crew's muffled swear come from under the hood, and she knew it was more than a seal. Slamming down the hood, he walked back to the window on the driver's side and reached in to pet Sam, who was dancing excitedly on the seat, wanting to get out.

Alexia looked at Crew expectantly.

"It's not good. The transmission fluid drains out as fast as I pour it in. I must have blown the pump," he explained.

"What do we do now?" she asked, pushing back the limp strands of hair that were clinging to her perspiring face.

"We walk."

"Walk?"

"Yeah, you know like in put one foot in front of the other."

"You're kidding, right... It's a hundred degrees in the shade, and I don't even have a rubber band to put my hair up..."

"You got a better idea?"

"Couldn't *he* go for help?" she asked, nodding to Sam.

Sam barked his enthusiasm for the idea.

"Shut up, Sam. You were lost when I found you."

Sam lay down on the seat and put his paws over his eyes and whined once.

"You could go for help," she said brightly.

"No way. I'm not leaving you alone out here on this deserted road. It might be dark before I could get help."

"Sam could protect me."

"Yeah, maybe. But I'm not taking any chances. You're both coming with me."

"I'm not helpless you know," she fumed.

"Look, I don't care how many aerobics classes you've taken, you're never a match for a man's strength."

She narrowed her eyes. "How do you know I take aerobics classes?"

"Uh . . . I . . . ah . . . don't. You just look like you're in pretty good shape."

"Oh." She looked away from the masculine compliment in his eyes.

"Let's see, I need to find something I can use as a leash for Sam. He chases anything that moves."

"Like his master, no doubt," Alexia muttered.

"What's that?" Crew asked, preoccupied with finding something to use for a leash.

"I just said I don't know how I'm going to walk any distance in these high heels and tight skirt."

"I suppose I could carry you piggyback," he offered.

"I'll walk, thank you," she said, jumping down from the truck and slamming the door.

While he was busy searching for a leash, she tried to surreptitiously remove her panty hose, not wanting to ruin them walking on the asphalt road.

She had just hiked up her narrow skirt when she heard his voice disturbingly near. "Need any help?"

"No! Stay where you are and don't look."

"Why? What are you doing?"

"Just never mind."

She finished what she was doing, not daring to look to see where exactly he was as she stepped out of her panty hose and slipped them into her jacket pocket. Smoothing down her skirt, she joined him.

His eyes swept over her. "I could have helped you, you know. I'm *real* good at taking off ladies' stockings."

"You looked!"

He grinned, offering no confirmation nor denial, merely saying, "I know naked legs when I see 'em."

Dear Editor:

Alexia has got Crew talking to his dog while she's *dating this Colby person, even though I suspect she is beginning to like Crew more than she lets on. But at the moment, I think she's planning to kill Crew. Is it too late for this to be a murder mystery instead of a romance?*

Tiffany

5

It got worse. Crew found something to use as a leash for Sam, all right—a huge coil of plastic rope he kept in the bed of his truck in case he needed it to tie anything down. After fastening one end of the rope around Sam's neck, he gave the dog a pat on the head and a generous lead, hoping he would behave. Crew then had to hold the huge coil of excess rope in his hand as he didn't have a knife with which to cut it.

The look on Alexia's face told him it was just as well there wasn't anything handy that even remotely resembled a weapon. She shook her head as she began walking alongside the disreputable looking pair.

Crew was wearing jams in a bright pattern containing at least sixteen different colors. If that weren't bad enough, he'd somehow managed to put on a pullover shirt that didn't match any of the sixteen different shades in his jams.

And between her and Crew was a dog on an ugly plastic rope.

It was a scene out of her worst nightmare. As a child she'd been so poor her dresses had been patched and her shoes taped to hold them together. She knew what it was to be laughed at.

After about a mile of walking in the stultifying heat, the trio looked even sorrier. Alexia was so miserable she didn't even care that she was trailing her jacket on the road, ruining it. Even the shoes she was carrying were growing heavy.

And perchance, should anyone going by not take note of the trio, Sam would make sure they did by barking at every bird, butterfly and critter they came across.

Alexia was thankful the only vehicles that passed them were dump trucks on their way to the dump located a mile or so from the park. A few of the drivers leaned out the window to whistle or catcall.

She stole a look over at Crew.

He was watching her and grinning. *Grinning!*

He actually thought their predicament was amusing. How could he? Was he completely insensitive?

"My offer of a piggyback ride still stands," he said, bravely ignoring the daggers her eyes were shooting at him.

Alexia blew the limp strands of hair out of her eyes and glared at him. "I am hot, sweaty, tired, embarrassed and furious, Mr. Harper. What I am not is amused."

Crew began laughing, ignoring her ill humor. "Aw, come on now, sweetheart. You've got to admit we make a pretty funny sight, the three of us. Why, if a person didn't know better he'd think we all just fell off the turnip truck on our first trip into the big city."

Alexia looked at him and Sam. Even if someone did come by, no one would offer them a ride with a dog along. It *was* pretty funny, and she bit the insides of her cheeks to still the laughter Crew was coaxing from her. But a moment later the laughter erupted, and Sam began jumping and barking, joining in their merriment.

Alexia finally got control of herself. "It's not funny," she sniffed.

"Aw, you're not going to cry are you? I don't know what to do with women who cry."

"I'm *not* crying," she said, wiping the tears with the back of her hands and marching on ahead of him.

"It won't be too much farther. I see something up ahead. Maybe we can stop and use their phone to call a cab."

"A cab? What about a tow truck?"

"Nah, I'll have the truck taken care of later. First I want to get you home."

They were sunburned, parched, dusty and dripping perspiration when they reached the building Crew had seen in the distance. It was an automobile dealership. But not just any automobile dealership. No, it had to be one of those that dealt in exclusive and expensive European sports cars. Just perfect, Alexia grumbled to herself. Why couldn't it have been a mirage.

As they trudged onto the parking lot, Alexia groaned when she saw the sleek green Jag that pulled past them and parked at the entrance to the showroom. The man who got out wore a suit that was obviously custom tailored and Italian loafers that must have cost three hundred dollars—no doubt the price without the tassels. He went around to help a stunning blonde out of the passenger side of the low-slung car.

"A friend of yours?" Crew asked, noticing her interest.

"No . . ." But she did know who he was. Colby had introduced them at the Regional Commerce and Growth Association meeting he'd taken her to.

"I didn't think so. He's not your type. A little too polished to be real, don't you think."

"How do you know what my type is? Besides, I hardly think anyone is going to look at me in my present state," she sputtered, gesturing down to indicate her damp blouse, rumpled skirt and dusty feet. "I don't exactly look like that dishy blonde he had on his arm."

"Dishy? Is that what she was. Well, I prefer you. I think you look fetching."

"Fetching . . ." She supposed that was meant to be a compliment. "Look, I know I look a mess. Could we please just get out of here."

"Oh, yeah, sure. Why don't you go on inside and make the call and I'll wait out here with Sam," Crew said, reaching into his pocket for change in case they had a pay phone.

"No!"

"Oh. Okay, well then I'll go inside and make the call, but you're going to have to hold on to Sam's leash," he said, handing over the coil of plastic rope.

While Crew strolled inside to make the call, not looking the least bit uncomfortable about his appearance, Alexia tugged Sam over to some shade beneath a tree away from the showroom windows. She didn't want anyone to see her looking the way she did. Once she was out of view, she flopped onto the ground with a weary sigh.

"Sam, I feel sorry for you, boy. Couldn't you have found a better master? Someone a little less... bohemian?"

Sam whined a few times in Crew's defense, it seemed, and then lay down beside her on the grass, resting his long nose on her leg. She didn't even realize she was petting him absently when Crew returned with two cold sodas.

"I see you two have made friends," he commented, handing her a cold can of soda she would have paid a hundred dollars for.

She was halfway through chugging it down her parched throat before she noticed Crew wasn't drinking his own. Instead he was pouring his soda into his cupped hand for Sam.

Feeling guilty and selfish, she slowed down gulping hers in case Crew didn't have any of his soda left over for himself.

"I ran into a bit of luck inside," Crew informed her with a smile when Sam finished lapping soda from Crew's cupped palm.

"They have a tow truck?"

"Better. Your friend's here picking up his car. It was in for its annual maintenance. He offered us a ride."

"Colby's here?" Alexia asked, both happy and miserable at hearing the news.

She looked to Crew for confirmation and sure enough he nodded.

"But what about Sam?"

"Oh, Sam prefers riding in a pickup truck, sure, but he'll ride in a fancy car if he has to."

"That's *not* what I meant."

"Maybe Colby won't notice Sam," Crew said with a wink.

"Who's Sam?" Colby asked, pulling up beside them.

Sam barked as Crew opened the passenger door and ushered Alexia into the air-conditioned car.

Colby's eyes widened, viewing her disheveled state up close. "Good grief, Alexia, you look a mess. Are you all right?"

"What she is, is hot, sweaty, tired, embarrassed and furious with me. What she's not, is amused," Crew answered for her, trying to coax a smile from her, knowing how mortified she was to have Colby see her in such a state.

It didn't work.

"Will you just get in," Alexia ground out between clenched teeth.

"Oh, I'm not coming along. Sam and I are going to take care of getting a tow truck for the pickup. Colby's going to take you home for me." With a wave he stepped back from the car and said, "I'll see you later."

"Don't count on it," she grumbled as Colby pushed the power button to close the window.

Crew tugged Sam's leash and headed back to the service area of the dealership to see about a tow truck.

"She's just pretending to be mad, Sam. Really, she likes me. She likes me a lot, don't you think?"

Sam barked, voicing his doubt.

"Shut up, Sam."

ALEXIA SAT AT HER DESK in her bedroom staring at the blank piece of paper in front of her, her mind not on the amusement park account, but on the man in her backyard digging her fish pond.

Crew had made what should have been a humiliating experience almost seem like fun. Or he'd tried to.

She'd never admit it to him, but she was the one at fault for ruining their trip to the park two nights ago. When his pickup had broken down on their way out of the park, it had been she who had put a pall on the evening by refusing to see the humor in the sight they'd made: a woman in a business suit walking barefoot beside what looked like a California beach bum and his dog on a rope.

If she were honest with herself, she had to admit it was she who had a problem, not he. But she was who she was. Growing up with ridicule had left her with a determination never to be poor and laughed at again. Couldn't he see she was harder on herself than anyone?

She rubbed her eyes with her hands as if she could wipe his image from her mind. She had to ignore his lazy grin that called her impulsive side out to play like a truant conspirator. The side of her too easily led astray. The side of her that could keep her from reaching her goals of success. Giving herself a stern lecture, she settled in to work on the account.

Though she worked steadily for several hours, no great inspiration came to her. The Funland Amusement Park was the most recalcitrant account she'd ever worked on. Ideas usually came so easily to her, but she couldn't get the one special angle she needed to nail the account.

Deciding to take a break, she went to the kitchen to make some lemonade. She stood at the sink looking out the window through the miniblinds as she squeezed lemons taken from the refrigerator. As she stirred a cup of sugar into the batch of lemonade, she watched the play of Crew's muscles as he worked at digging the hole in her backyard for the fish pond she'd bartered for her advertising services.

Bare chested and sweat slicked, he stopped from time to time to wipe his hands down the thighs of his soft, worn jeans with the knees out. Hands she remembered had calluses from hard work. Despite his good looks, Crew Harper was no pretty boy.

She felt guilty working inside in the air conditioning while he toiled away out in the noonday sun.

She'd missed seeing him Thursday and Friday evening when he hadn't shown up because his pickup was being repaired. She didn't like it at all that she'd missed him. Didn't like the fact that when he was around, her thoughts and eyes were drawn to him. Didn't like it that he had her peeking out half-shuttered blinds like some repressed spinster lady.

She sighed, tapping the wooden spoon on the pitcher of lemonade when she finished stirring. It had been so long since she'd allowed herself to have fun. Sometimes she couldn't even remember when the last time had been. No, that wasn't exactly true. She had the tattoo to remind her. Remind her of her folly.

Pushing the memory from her mind, she filled two tall glasses with ice and lemonade and carried them outside. She stood for a moment at the edge of the twenty-by-twenty hole Crew was digging just watching him. He must have felt her watching him, because he looked over to where she stood.

"I see you got your truck fixed," she said, able to see the disreputable hulk from her backyard.

"Yeah, and not a moment too soon," he said with a chuckle.

"What's that? Surely you didn't miss coming over here and digging in this heat?" She blushed, realizing it sounded like she was fishing.

He just looked at her funny, then said, "Actually I was referring to Sam. He was starting to like riding around in a fancy car, weren't you boy?"

Sam paid no attention, just kept digging at a root in the spaded ground.

"Fancy car?" Alexia said, puzzled.

"That's all that place had to rent me."

"Oh." He'd had a car...he could have come by. Why hadn't he? she wondered. Had he been squiring some dishy blonde around in that fancy car as well as Sam?

"If you wore a T-shirt, you wouldn't be getting that sunburn," she said, then wished she hadn't because it gave away the fact that she was looking at him.

He paused in his digging, a half smile ghosting his lips. "I bother you, don't I?"

"Excuse me?"

"The fact that I'm not afraid of you," he explained with a shrug of those very wide sunburned shoulders.

"Afraid of me?" she repeated incredulously. "What on earth are you talking about?"

"That act of yours. It doesn't scare me off, you know," he said, jamming the shovel into the earth with his foot. "I bet you've got old Colby dancing a pretty tune with it, though, don't you?"

"Act? What act?" she demanded, watching him toss the spade of dirt over his bare shoulder.

He stopped shoveling and leaned forward, bracing his sweaty sinewy forearms on the handle of the shovel. A trickle of sweat slid from his temple onto his unshaven jaw. "You know good and well what act," he drawled in a bedroom whisper, dropping the shovel and ambling over toward her.

"No! No, I don't," she answered, recovering her composure by shoving the glass of lemonade at him. She'd made the drink to cool his thirst, though the hot look in his eyes didn't cry out for liquid to slake it.

He stared at her consideringly, then took a long thirsty swallow of the tart drink, draining the glass. When he was done, he wiped his lips with his forearm, and handed the empty glass back to her.

"What's the matter, Alexia. Hasn't any man ever seen through your act before? Am I the first?"

"You're talking gibberish," Alexia said, turning on her heel to flee to the safety of the house, away from amber eyes that saw too much.

"Am I?" he whispered after her, the question sending goose bumps up her spine.

She hesitated the briefest of moments.

"You're a control freak, Alexia," he said. "Why is that do you suppose? Is it because you're afraid of what you might do if you gave in to your impulses? Afraid you might let loose your feelings . . . desires, if only for a moment like you did on the dance floor of the honky-tonk?"

She didn't answer him, fleeing to the house instead. Once inside, she returned to the desk in her bedroom and the Funland Amusement Park account, losing herself in the safety of the work.

Hours passed and she was so lost in her work that at first she didn't hear Crew come in when he was done for the day. She jumped when he spoke from her bedroom doorway.

"Is that my account you're working on? Can I come see what you've come up with?"

Startled out of her deep concentration, she placed a hand on her chest to calm her racing heart. "No," she replied. "I'm working on the Funland Amusement Park account."

"Oh. How's it going?"

"It's not," she said on a sigh.

He nodded. "You ever been there?" he asked, his eyes sliding around her bedroom, taking it all in from the oversize lounge chair in wide pink-and-white stripes to the lace tablecloth recruited as window drapery.

"Yes. I've been there a time or two since I got the account."

"By yourself?"

She nodded.

"Well, that's the problem right there. You don't go to amusement parks alone. Why don't you live a little. Let me show you how to have a real good time," he dared.

When she didn't respond, he coaxed, "You never know, it might be downright inspiring—give you an angle you're overlooking . . ."

He had a point, she decided. She wasn't getting anywhere sitting at her desk no matter how hard she tried to concentrate.

Maybe a trip to the amusement park *would* give her some ideas. She'd go to most any length to secure the account and thus a partnership in Gund & Associates. Well, almost any length.

"Okay, but it's not a date," she was quick to point out. "It's just research."

"Whatever you say."

"What time?"

Crew looked down at his watch. "I'll have to take Sam home and shower. Say around eight?"

"Okay," she agreed, already beginning to doubt the wisdom of her decision as a mental image of Crew showering flashed through her mind. She really was going to have to break this daydreaming habit she'd developed. It was interfering with her work and she couldn't allow anything—or anyone—to do that.

Crew's eyes twinkled as they swept over her large pencil-post bed enveloped with yards of mosquito netting. "You get a lot of pests in here, do you?" he asked, tongue firmly planted in cheek.

"Out!" Alexia ordered, pointing the way.

She heard him chuckling as he headed through the kitchen, then went outside.

Her back was to the door as she gathered up the papers on her desk when she heard his footsteps return. She turned to see him in the doorway.

"I almost forgot," he said, raising his hand and tossing a package on the soft cushy chair. "That's for you."

He vanished from her doorway before she could object. By the time she got her voice, she heard him whistle for Sam then the sound of the pickup pulling away from the curb.

"What on earth..." she muttered, staring at the pretty package as if it were a coiled snake. No one had ever given her a present before.

When she'd been growing up there hadn't been money for such luxuries, even at Christmas. Later, she'd never allowed anyone to get close enough.

Alexia approached the chair, staring down at the package. Were there invisible strings attached? she wondered.

Finally curiosity, and if she were honest, secret delight compelled her to pick it up. The slim box was white with a shimmery gold cord bow tied around it. The name of an exclusive lingerie shop was embossed in gold on the lid of the box. There was a small card tucked under the gold cord tie and she slipped it free.

Dear Alexia—

Sorry about the other night.

Crew

With a puzzled frown, she tossed the card on the chair and slowly slid the gold cord tie from around the box, opening the lid while remembering the night the pickup had broken down.

When she pulled open the tissue, she revealed a pair of creamy high-cut French panty hose with a lace top. They were an exact match to the kind she wore. Crew *had* peeked when she'd removed her panty hose beside the truck.

He was a rat. A smile touched her lips as she fingered her first present. *But a very sweet rat.*

Dear Editor:

You'll be glad to know Crew is shaping up and I believe he's actually managed to storm some of Alexia's defenses. Things are actually going rather swimmingly at the moment.

Tiffany

6

ALEXIA WIPED THE STEAM from her bathroom mirror after her shower so she could apply her makeup. As she studied her face in the mirror, she remembered Colby's words of advice when he'd driven her home after Crew's pickup had broken down earlier in the week. Colby had said that as her friend he felt he should warn her that clients would judge her by the company she kept, and that while Crew Harper certainly seemed a nice enough guy, he just wasn't their sort.

Their sort.

If Colby only knew. Knew she was a pretender. Knew the amount of effort it took to keep up the pretense. She lived in fear that her charade would be discovered and all her hopes for a secure future would tumble like a house of cards.

Maybe once she made partner with the amusement park account, she would be able to relax. Then she would belong. But until then, no one must find out that she hadn't gone to the right schools, hadn't in fact gone to any school at all.

Maybe that was why she was so comfortable with Crew. With him she didn't feel the pressure to measure up. He made her feel... No, she didn't want to think about how he made her feel.

A half hour later she was dressed in a short, narrow denim skirt, a pair of ostrich-print cowboy boots and a cream-colored soft cotton top with a wide neck that tended to slip off one smooth shoulder. As she did a turn before the full-length mirror in her bedroom, she tried to tell herself she'd dressed for comfort, but she knew the short skirt and boots emphasized her long legs.

Legs Crew noticed right off when he arrived, signaling his approval with a construction-worker wolf whistle.

"Boy, you sure don't make it easy on a guy, do you?"

"What do you mean?"

"You expect me to pretend you're not my date when you look that hot."

"I do not look hot!"

"If you say so."

"Could we go now?" Alexia asked.

Picking up a tiny purse, she slung the strap over her shoulder, and for the first time since he arrived, she looked directly at Crew. She nearly choked when she read the printing on the T-shirt he wore with a pair of new jeans. The logo looked at first like one from a popular café, but upon closer scrutiny it read Rock Hard. She headed for the car, not daring to comment.

Crew switched off the radio when he started the pickup and they rode in silence for a while. It wasn't a comfortable silence exactly because the cab was filled with the sounds of their breathing, a close sexy atmosphere.

"So you did look after all," Alexia finally said, bringing up the present he'd bought her.

Crew glanced over at her and grinned. "I'm not Colby Langston," he said, pulling into a parking space on the lot of the amusement park and cutting the engine. Opening the door he went around to assist her out of the pickup, his eyes glancing off her flash of legs as he offered her his hand.

"I was wondering..." he said as they walked to the entrance of the amusement park, "do you ever wear those other kind?"

"Other kind?"

"Yeah, the real sexy black ones with the seams up the back."

Alexia sighed.

"Guess not, huh? Good thing I didn't buy those, this being our first date and all," he teased.

"This is not a date!"

"Right. Sorry, I keep forgetting," Crew apologized looking more wolfish than sheepish.

He did, however, insist on paying their way in.

"Let's go on my favorite ride first," he said, taking her hand.

Reluctantly she let him guide her through the crowd to the ride.

"You're kidding," she said upon seeing it.

"Nah, come on. It'll be fun."

Fun. That was what she was afraid of as she looked at the hearts and flowers entrance to the Tunnel of Love.

"I don't think this is such a good idea," she said, stepping back.

Crew turned and rested his forearms on her shoulders. A party atmosphere whirled all around them—the boisterous laughter of the jostling crowd, the aroma of hot-buttered popcorn and fried apple fritters, the tinny music from all the different rides clashing in a noisy cacophony, while the gaudy colors of neon lights flashed on and off. Looking into her eyes, Crew reduced it to just the two of them.

"I think it's a real good idea," he said, touching his forehead on hers, peering into her eyes. His warm breath caressed her cheek as he promised, "I'll be good . . . I won't leave more than one hicky on your neck. . . ."

Her eyes widened and he laughed out loud, grabbing her hand playfully. "Come on, Alexia, loosen up . . . have some fun."

Alexia allowed herself to be tugged along in Crew's wake. She'd never been in a tunnel of love and had no idea of what to expect. Not that one ever would know what to expect with Crew at the helm, she suspected.

Crew bought their ride tickets, then slid his arm along the back of the seat as the attendant closed the crossbar on the little railcar. The ride started with a jerk and the railcar went through a swinging door at the entrance of the tunnel.

"Oh, my . . ." Alexia whispered as pitch-blackness enveloped them.

"Yeah, it's neat, isn't it," Crew said, letting his hand drop and curve around her bare shoulder where the cotton top had slipped.

Alexia stiffened at his touch.

"Relax," Crew coaxed. "Pretend we're sweethearts and enjoy the ride. You're not going to get any ideas for your presentation if you don't get into the spirit of things."

Alexia forced herself to relax. She supposed Crew was right. It wouldn't hurt to pretend.

She tried to ignore the frisson of excitement his thumb created, however, as he rubbed it in sensual circles on her bare shoulder. The railcar took them around a corner and the pitch-black was illuminated suddenly by a soft glow from the romantic waterfall they passed beneath.

When they were surrounded by darkness once again, Crew asked, "Did you and Colby meet in school or have your families always known each other?"

"I didn't meet Colby until he came to work for Gund & Associates about a year ago."

"Then you don't know him all that well. You wouldn't for instance be able to tell if he was trying to sabotage your work in any way?"

"What?" she asked as they passed a huge backlit cupid. Why was he suggesting Colby would do such a thing, she wondered. Did he know something? No, he was merely trying to drive a wedge between her and Colby, she decided. *Men.*

"His line about not being competitive could be a hoax."

"It's not. Colby's introduced me to lots of potential clients. He wouldn't do that if he were trying to sabotage my work. I don't have to worry about Colby."

In the darkness she couldn't see the look of doubt on Crew's face.

Crew inched closer on the seat beside her, their bodies touching shoulder to knee.

"You, however, I do have to worry about," Alexia said, lifting his arm off her shoulder and scooting away from the lure of his warm body.

"Me? I was just cold. Don't you feel a chill in here?"

"Nice try," she said as they passed a flowery display.

"You don't believe me?"

"Isn't this ride almost over?"

"I don't think we get to leave until we kiss."

"What?"

"Yeah, somehow they can tell and they don't pass you through the hidden exit until you kiss your partner."

"That's ridiculous."

"Come on, Alexia, just one little kiss . . ." There was repressed laughter in his voice.

"I'm not coming near you."

The railcar turned a corner and a giant monster popped up out of the water with a roar, its eyes glowing red in the dark.

Alexia jumped into Crew's lap and threw her arms around him with a scream.

Crew cradled her in his arms, chuckling. "Don't worry. I'll protect you for a kiss."

"You! You knew about the monster," she accused, glaring at him as the monster receded back into the water and darkness enveloped them once again.

"What else is going to happen?" she asked leeringly.

"If you give me a kiss, I might tell you," he whispered sending shivery tingles down her spine.

"Might . . . ?"

"Okay, give me a kiss and I *will* tell you," he said, chuckling, "Scout's honor, promise."

"I'm beginning to believe you negotiated all your scouting badges," she said with a sniff.

"My kiss . . ." he reminded, ignoring her jibe.

She sighed, then halfheartedly tried planting a platonic peck on his cheek.

"Uh-uh."

"What?"

"That was a kiss for children or maiden aunts, and I'm neither. I want a *real* kiss. A kiss that gets my attention. *A kiss like this...*" he insisted, lowering his lips and brushing them against hers provocatively as he pulled her close.

She opened her mouth to protest and he took full advantage, settling his open mouth over hers. His breath was warm and his tongue firm and sure as it thrust, exploring and tasting her with exciting intimacy. His thumbs brushed the sensitive undersides of her arms, and Alexia tried to temper her response to his sensual assault. But he stormed her defenses with his addictive, hypnotic caress, stripping away the surface layers of her reserve.

He kissed her with an effortless expertise. Every thrust and parry of his tongue was laced with a skilled authority...coaxing, ever so persuasively, until she was kissing him back with unreserved abandon.

"Aw right! Yo, Momma!"

Alexia was startled out of her sensual lassitude by the catcalls and whistles. Her eyes flew open to see they had exited the Tunnel of Love and were outside at the entrance where others waited their turn.

"You knew!" she accused, her face flaming bright red with embarrassment.

"I forgot. You got me all . . . I forgot."

When the ride attendant let them out of the railcar, she stomped away to a chorus of laughter from the surrounding crowd.

"Alexia!" Crew called after her, but she didn't stop.

He had to sprint to catch up to her.

She glared at him.

He took her hand. "Here, let's go in here until you calm down and relax," he suggested, coaxing her with his apology. "I'm sorry, really. I didn't think you'd get so upset over a little O.D.A."

"O.D.A?" Alexia asked, allowing him to lead her into the fun house of mirrors.

"Overt Display of Affection," Crew explained, hugging her as they looked in the distorted mirror that made them look short and wide. It was impossible not to laugh at the images they made in the fun house mirrors and by the time they exited, her anger had faded.

"Let's get something to eat," Crew suggested as they walked by a corn dog stand.

They washed the corn dogs down with sodas and then he bought a big cotton candy for them to share.

"You've got some there..." Crew informed her when she'd taken a few bites of the airy pink sweet confection.

"Where?"

"Right there," Crew said, leaning close and licking the bit of cotton candy from her cheek.

"You're not angry with me anymore, are you?" he whispered in her ear.

To her chagrin, she was finding it impossible to stay angry with him for any length of time. "No, I suppose not," she answered, wishing his nearness didn't make her feel so . . . so restless somehow.

"Good."

They strolled down the midway, Crew resting his arm on her shoulder as he fed her bits of cotton candy. "What do you want to do now?" he asked, tossing the last of the cotton candy in the receptacle when they'd had their fill.

Alexia looked around, dazzled by the array of choices. "I don't know. Let's just walk around for a while," she suggested, noting Crew hadn't removed his arm from her shoulder. He wasn't doing a very good job of remembering this wasn't a date.

Up ahead on their left, a crowd was gathered around a little platform in front of a bright blue tent. Spying it, Alexia pointed and said, "Let's go over there and see what's going on."

"Okay," Crew agreed, steering her toward it. When they reached the edge of the crowd, Alexia saw it was a belly dancer in gold bangles and bright floaty veils who had captured the crowd's attention. She was exotic and attractive and really quite good. How did she make her body move so provocatively? Alexia wondered, casting a covert glance Crew's way.

He was smiling his appreciation up at the dancer and appeared to be settling in for the duration of her performance. Alexia tugged his arm to get his attention. "I know what I want to do now."

Crew looked over at her. "Learn to belly dance?" he asked, a hopeful gleam in his eye.

"Uh-uh."

"Shame . . ." he said, shaking his head then glancing back up at the dancer.

Alexia fumed and tugged his arm again. "I want to have my fortune told."

Crew tore his attention away from the dancer. "No problem," he said. "*I* can tell your fortune. You're going to meet a tall . . . okay, sort of tall, dark and *very* handsome man." He grinned big time as he spread his arms wide. "Voilà! Am I good, or what?"

Alexia sighed. "I don't care about romance, silly."

"You don't?"

She shook her head.

"Then what . . ."

"My career," she informed him as if he were dense. "What I want to know about is my career."

"Oh, that." Crew shrugged his wide shoulders. "I can predict that, too." His amber eyes seemed to glow as his voice deepened and he said, "You are going to meet a tall—he's tall, satisifed—but he's not very dark." Smiling wickedly, he continued. "In fact, he's sort of a pastel kind of guy, if you know what I mean. And he's definitely *not* handsome. You must beware of this man for he will try to trick you."

Alexia snorted. "That's about as transparent as Miss D Cup Bangle's veils," she said, nodding toward the dancer on the platform. "Now can we please go and see the *real* fortune teller I saw on the way in."

"Real fortune teller, eh? What's she got that I don't?" Crew grumbled, allowing her to lead him away from the gyrating dancer on the platform.

"Crystal balls," Alexia answered, not looking over when she heard him choke.

"I DON'T LIKE THE LOOKS of this at all," Crew muttered when they reached the fortune teller's tent. The hand-lettered sign propped on an easel outside the tent read:

FORTUNE TELLING
PALM READING
TAROT CARDS

"Which of the three bothers you?" Alexia asked, surprised he was superstitious.

"None," Crew answered, pointing instead to the name below the fortune teller's picture.

Alexia squinted, reading the name out loud, "Madam Rose?"

Crew nodded. "I'm allergic, remember?"

Alexia shrugged. "Good, then you can wait outside."

"Not on your life," Crew replied, pulling the tent flap open and ushering her inside.

The inside of the tent was lit only with candles, whose flickering flames made eerie shapes on the canvas. Strange music played on a skipping record and a spicy fragrance drifting on the air lent an exotic atmosphere.

Crew walked over and rang the bell sitting on the folding table half-covered with a triangle of paisley material in a rich, dark texture.

Madam Rose appeared a few moments later.

She was tall and imposing in a bright purple caftan, a fringed silky shawl bunched in her hands. Gold jewelry shone in abundance. Large gold hoops swung from her ears, and when she sat down at the card table, her gold bracelets jangled.

Taking a crystal ball from beneath the silky shawl in her hands, she set it before them on the table. She motioned for them to be seated opposite her.

When they were seated, she waved her hands over the crystal ball while waiting for the cloudy mist to clear. Each finger on her long slender hands was beringed.

"What is it you want, my dear?" Madam Rose asked, looking to Alexia.

"How do you know she's the one who wants something?" Crew demanded, not cottoning to being ignored by the two women.

"She reads minds...." Alexia said with a pained sigh.

"Oh. Right."

Madam Rose hid a smile and peered into the crystal ball. "I see some sort of deception," the fortune teller began.

"That's exactly what I've been trying to tell her," Crew said impatiently.

Madam Rose nodded. Looking into her crystal ball again, she said, "Yes, I see a dark-haired man."

"What?" Crew asked incredulously.

Madam Rose shrugged. "A dark-haired man," she repeated.

"No, no, no. You've gotten it all wrong. It's a fair-haired man who's trying to deceive her," Crew insisted. "Look again, he wears a lot of pastels."

Madam Rose looked into her crystal ball again. She shook her head. "No, it's clearly a dark-haired man who is hiding something from her."

"What? What is he hiding?" Alexia asked.

Madam Rose glanced over at the upset young man. Crew caught her eye and rubbed his fingers together signaling he would pay money for her silence.

Madam Rose made a barely perceptible nod and peered into the crystal ball once again. She looked up at Alexia after a moment and shook her head. "I'm sorry. I'm afraid it's gone. All the argument must have disturbed the spirits."

Alexia turned on Crew. "Now see what you've done," she accused.

"Me?" Crew replied, looking as innocent as a two-year-old just awakened from a restful nap.

"Never mind," Alexia said, knowing that pursuing his guilt was hopeless.

"Maybe she could read your palm," Crew suggested, wanting to distract Alexia from the fortune teller's message. He didn't really believe the fortune teller knew he was hiding something from Alexia. Knew that he had watched Alexia undress in her office. But if

Alexia were to find out about it, she'd never have anything to do with him.

"Good idea," Alexia agreed, turning back to Madam Rose and offering up her palm.

Madam Rose took Alexia's palm. Flattening it out, she studied it carefully, her sharp eyes missing nothing. "What is it you wish to know about?" she asked.

"My career. I want to know about my career."

"She wants to be a partner," Crew said.

"A partner? Is this true?" Madam Rose asked Alexia.

Alexia nodded.

Madam Rose looked down at Alexia's palm again, continuing to study it. "You will have your wish. Yes, I see clearly that you will be a partner if that is what you wish . . ."

Alexia smiled widely.

"But," the fortune teller warned, "you will also have to make a choice."

"I don't understand . . ." Alexia said, clearly puzzled.

A warm breeze blew at the tent flap as Madam Rose looked deeply into her eyes. "You will soon have to make a decision about the path your life will take. There is a fork in your hand . . . Either choice will bring you the success you desire as there is luck in your hand. You have a star on the pad of your palm. But only one choice will bring you happiness."

"But how will I know . . . ?" Alexia began.

Madam Rose folded Alexia's hand, sheltering it in the warmth of her own. "You must learn to trust yourself, my dear."

Withdrawing her hand, Madam Rose looked over at Crew. "How about you, young man. Do you wish me to read your palm for you?"

"No," he answered quickly, pulling his hand into his lap beneath the table.

"Your fortune then?"

"Come on, do it," Alexia coaxed. "That or the tarot cards."

"My fortune," Crew chose, not liking the look of the foreboding tarot cards.

"You also wish to know about your career?" the fortune teller asked.

"Hell no, tell me something juicy about my love life," he suggested with a wink.

Madam Rose waved her hands back and forth over the crystal ball muttering a few indistinguishable phrases beneath her breath.

Peering into the crystal ball at last, she shook her head. "It doesn't look good," she said.

"What? Let me have a look at that," Crew said, jumping up.

Alexia tugged on his arm, pulling him back into his chair.

"You will only have one love in your life," the fortune teller continued.

"So, what's wrong with that?" Crew demanded, to Alexia's surprise.

"Nothing, if it works. But it means you will only have one chance at personal happiness."

"Guess I'd better not screw up then. What's the name of the love of my life?"

The fortune teller shook her head.

"Initials. I'll settle for initials."

She just looked at him.

"Well, how am I supposed to know?" Crew asked in exasperation.

"You will know," Madam Rose said, patting his hand.

"What about his business?" Alexia asked. "He's starting up a new business. I'm going to help him launch it. Will it be a success?"

"For that I need to see your palm," Madam Rose said, looking to Crew who offered his hand to her reluctantly.

Tracing the lines on his palm with her forefinger, she shook her head. "You have not had much good fortune in your life," she commented. Tracing further, she brightened. "But all that might change. There is opportunity in your hand and a chance to do well."

"A chance, you say?"

Madam Rose nodded.

"Well, then, I can't complain, can I? How much do I owe you, Madam Rose?"

"No, this was my idea," Alexia insisted pulling her wallet from her tiny shoulder bag and handing over the sum Madam Rose named.

Crew pressed an additional bill into the fortune teller's hand with a wink, explaining to Alexia that it was merely a tip.

"Now what shall we do?" Alexia asked as they left the tent and strolled down the midway. Hucksters on both sides called to them, plying their games of chance. "If you were a real gentleman, I suppose you'd win me a stuffed animal," she hinted, eyeing the big white panda bear.

"I'll win you one anyway," Crew said.

Dear Editor:

I don't believe it. Alexia didn't melt in Crew's arms in the Tunnel of Love. I swear she is the most stubborn, mule headed, obstinate . . .

This isn't going at all the way I planned.

Tiffany

7

SLIPPING HIS HAND into the front pocket of his tight jeans, Crew inched several quarters out and laid them on the wooden ledge fronting the shooting gallery. He picked up the rifle, then nodded to the attendant behind the counter who started up a line of little wooden duck targets. Crew took aim as they sailed past and won the panda bear Alexia craved on the first try, much to the attendant's chagrin.

Settling the panda bear in Alexia's arms, he said, "Now we can discuss just how you're going to reward me for winning this for you."

"A gentleman wouldn't ask for a reward."

Crew just looked at her.

"Okay, I'll let you choose what we do next," she offered.

"Great idea," he said, his eyes sparkling with sensual fire.

"Uh-uh," she said, shaking her head. "It has to be something in the amusement park."

His eyes continued to sparkle nonetheless.

"And not the Tunnel of Love, either," she added, correctly guessing the direction of his thoughts.

"Spoilsport." He thought a moment then said, "Okay, follow me" as he took her hand.

She grumbled, but allowed him to lead as she followed in his wake until they came to his intended destination at the end of the midway.

"Bumper cars! I'm *not* getting in one of those. Oh, no, I'm not. Do you hear me, Crew Harper?"

"Aw, come on, Alexia. For once let down your guard and allow yourself to have some fun," he coaxed, the teasing light back in his eyes.

She could see there was nothing she could do but go along with what he wanted and ride the bumper cars. He could be the most stubborn human on earth sometimes, she thought. Glaring at him she said, "And what am I supposed to do with this stupid bear if I did get in one of the cars?" she asked, imperiously nodding to the panda he'd won her.

"I'll take care of the bear," Crew promised, lifting it from her hands and covering its ears. "You're not stupid," he said soothingly to the bear while pretending a chastising look at Alexia. "Don't pay her no mind, bear. She's just frustrated. What she needs is . . ." He deliberately didn't finish the sentence Alexia was straining to hear as he headed for the ticket booth.

When he came back, he presented the ride attendant with three tickets and plopped the panda bear in a separate bumper car of its own to her astonishment and the delight of a watching youngster in pigtails.

Crew took the bumper car behind Alexia's. When the ride started, he began nudging Alexia's car from behind. From the corner of her eye, she could see the little girl giggling while she tried to bump her car into the bumper car containing the panda bear.

She was distracted from watching the child by a jolt to her own car that sent her sailing. "All right, I've had it with you, Crew Harper," she vowed under her breath. "You want a fight, you've got one." Turning her bumper car around when it came to a stop, she headed straight for Crew at full speed, her eyes filled with childish glee.

A frown replaced her grinning malice when Crew maneuvered out of her way.

"Rat!" She turned and headed for him again, but once more he managed to just skirt her approaching bumper car, getting out of her path of destruction.

Her face was filled with concentration as she chased him around the track. When she finally had him boxed in, she headed straight for him, her laughter rushing out in gales when she plowed into him, sending his car spinning crazily.

The ride was over before he got a chance to retaliate, but that didn't stop him. Getting out of his bumper car, he bore down on her, his muscular legs eating up the distance between their cars.

Laughing hysterically, Alexia jumped from her bumper car and grabbed the panda bear from its car, holding the bear in front of her for protection.

Crew continued to approach her, wriggling his fingers in a gesture that promised he'd tickle her senseless when he captured her. "I've got you now, my pretty," he called, closing in on her to exact his revenge.

Alexia shoved the panda bear at him. While he was grappling with the large bear, she turned and took off running.

"Look," the girl in pigtails alerted him, pointing after Alexia's retreating form.

"Oh, no, you don't," Crew called, taking off after Alexia in haphazard pursuit, his progress slowed by the large panda that kept threatening to slip from his arm. Jumping down from the side of the ride rather than taking the exit saved him steps.

Running was difficult. They were laughing so hard their sides hurt.

When he caught up to her, Crew pulled her into his strong arms.

"You're not going to tickle me," she said, trying to catch her breath.

"You deserve it."

"Why?"

"You indicated if I won the panda bear for you that you'd look kindly on me. Well, I won you the bear and so what did you do? Did you hug me? No. Did you kiss me? No. What you did was . . ."

"Bumped you off?" she supplied, smiling with pretended innocence.

"Exactly," he agreed with a grin.

"Well, you shouldn't frustrate me so much," she said by way of defense.

"Like you don't frustrate me."

As they gazed into each other's eyes, the laughter between them died down to be replaced by a shimmering heat. Crew pulled her up on her toes, taking her mouth with his, exacting a delicious brand of revenge that sent Alexia's emotions spinning as crazily as the Tilt-A-Whirl ride behind her.

When they broke apart, Alexia struggled to regain the wall of reserve his caress had stormed.

"If you don't stop these O.D.A.'s you're so overly fond of, you're going to find yourself D.O.A." she warned, breaking away from him completely and heading down the midway toward the exit.

With a few strides Crew reached her. Catching her arm, he spun her around to face him.

"Cut the crap, Alexia. You've had the time of your life tonight. Why can't you admit it? It might not be ritzy enough for you, but I've been watching you all night, and you've had fun in spite of yourself."

Alexia shrugged. "I suppose I did get some ideas I might be able to use in my presentation for the Funland account," she agreed, trying to keep the conversation between them impersonal, purposely avoiding what was really being said.

His fingers tightened on her upper arms where he gripped her. "Don't you *ever* forget about work?"

"What's wrong?" she asked, knowing the answer.

His face closed. "With me? Nothing," he answered, releasing her in disgust.

"Look, thanks for bringing me here tonight. I really do appreciate it."

"Yeah."

"WHY DO I BOTHER?" Crew swore, kicking the refrigerator shut with his bare foot.

Sam sat at his feet by the counter in the small kitchen of the trailer waiting for the leftover chili and nachos Crew was warming up at three o'clock in the morning.

"I bet *she's* sleeping like a baby," Crew grumbled, popping open a beer as he took the bubbling chili off the burner.

"What's wrong with me, Sam? Why am I trying to help a dame who looks down her nose at me? I must be an idiot!"

Sam barked as Crew split the pot of leftover chili between two bowls and set one on the floor before the dog who looked at him with soulful brown eyes.

"Shut up, Sam."

ALEXIA TOSSED AND TURNED beneath the mosquito netting on her bed. Raising herself on her elbows she looked over at the clock radio on the tall wicker lingerie chest. It was three in the morning.

She punched her pillow.

She hated Crew Harper. She really, really did.

WHEN ALEXIA GOT HOME from the market with the carton of milk she'd needed, she found Crew and Sam sitting on the front porch waiting for her arrival. Man and dog both had matching red farmer's kerchiefs tied around their necks.

"What are you doing out here on the porch?" Alexia asked, walking toward where they were sitting.

"I've come about the fish pond, of course," Crew answered, unfolding his lithe body with casual grace to stand when she reached them. Sam only roused himself to open one eye and look up at her from his prone position where he lay panting.

"Let me guess," she grumbled, opening the door. "You're going to be the scum on top, right?" She was cranky after a sleepless night.

"Now, now, is that any way to talk," Crew said, following her inside. Sam finally roused himself to scurry inside before the storm door swished shut, but just barely. It was a habit of his that drove Crew nuts.

"What about the pond?" Alexia asked over her shoulder, ignoring his question as she set the milk on the kitchen counter.

Crew lounged in the doorway. "Well, I wasn't sure if we still had a deal," he said. "We didn't part on the best of terms last night, you know."

She knew. They'd ridden home in silence and he'd left her—no, dumped her and the panda bear—at her front door with nary a word.

"I don't care. You can't just leave a dusty hole in my backyard."

"I could fill it back in."

"No."

"You're sure?"

"I'm sure."

"Well, then I'll go on out and get to work." He didn't move.

She nodded and turned her back to him.

"Right," he mumbled.

She heard the screen door slam as he went outside.

Alexia moved to her kitchen window and watched Crew and Sam at the site of the future fish pond. Crew peeled off his T-shirt and toed off his tennis shoes and began digging in the hard clay earth, while Sam lay in the sun and barked at every bird that dared to fly overhead no matter how high in the sky the bird flew.

Why does he bother with me at all? Alexia wondered, watching the play of Crew's muscles while he worked at digging a hole that never seemed to get any deeper. What was it Crew Harper really wanted? He had to have some hidden motive, because no matter how much grief she gave him, he kept coming back for more.

The sun took its toll on Crew as he worked. As she watched furtively from the window, his faded jeans became damp, molding to his strong thighs. Sweat glistened on his chest and back as he threw shallow shovels of dirt over his shoulder, his jeans slipping low on his hips.

With great reluctance Alexia tore herself away from the window. She had better things to do than spy on Crew like some lovesick fool. If she didn't come up with a great presentation for the Funland Amusement Park account, all the hard work she'd put into her career would be for naught.

And it had been hard work. Things had never come easily to her. She'd started as a secretary in an advertising firm straight out of high school. Applying herself, she'd taken courses in creative writing at the local junior college. When an opening came up for a junior copywriter, she'd convinced the company she was working for to give her a chance. There had been nothing glamorous about writing text for catalogs, but she'd given the work her best effort while continuing to take classes in the hope that an even better opportunity would come along.

It was while preparing a portfolio of sample ads for one of her classes that she found out about an advertising club that would critique her work. When she submitted her portfolio, the creative director who saw her work had liked it so much he'd recommended her to an associate of his at Gund & Associates.

Within six months she had been promoted to senior copywriter. She loved the job of coming up with innovative ideas to sell new products or update old ones. She only spent about ten percent of her time writing, the rest of her time was spent thinking.

Selling the client on the idea was the hard part of her job. She had to come up with an idea that would sell itself to get the partnership she so desperately wanted at Gund & Associates.

Once she had the partnership, she would belong. She wouldn't be an outsider anymore.

She tried to work. For hours she tried to work. But try as she might her mind wouldn't stay on the Funland Amusement Park account. Even when she tried to recall her visit to it, all she thought about was the bare chested man outside in her backyard digging the fish pond from hell. The fish pond that showed no signs of ever being finished. She might as well admit it to herself, that despite her best efforts at protecting herself from such a thing ever happening, Crew Harper seemed to have sweet-talked his way into her life . . . into her every waking thought . . . and if she wasn't very, very careful . . . into her bed.

She thought of the flames of desire that backlit his amber eyes, his wicked grin of delicious promise that dared her to succumb to its silent invitation...his body that wouldn't quit.

Maybe if she just slept with him . . .

No!

Was she crazy?

But . . . he couldn't possibly be as good in bed as she thought he was. If she slept with him . . .

No!

What on earth was wrong with her? She had to stop this nonsense. She had to stop thinking about him all the time. Stop seeing him in her mind's eye, even when she was trying to work. Stop yearning for the touch of his . . . Stop!

Throwing down her pencil in frustration, she buried her head of tousled caramel curls in her hands.

Once before she had done something really impulsive. And really dumb. It, too, had been inspired by a man. A man, or rather a boy really, who had paid attention to her. One who hadn't laughed at her—to her face, anyway, as it turned out.

Bradley Turner had been president of their senior class and on the track team. He was popular and dated all the prettiest girls in school, so she'd been flattered when he'd turned his attention to her.

Brad's real passion was collecting butterflies and she had shared his butterfly hunts with him. Racing through meadows with nets flying, she'd thought they had fallen in love.

It had been in a field of wildflowers that he'd made love to her, right after she'd captured a prize specimen for his ever growing butterfly collection. He had been a very possessive lover and her first. She'd had a fleeting feeling afterward that he'd wanted to stick a pin through her and add her to his collection, a prize to be displayed.

But she'd shaken off the feeling and on impulse as a sign of her devotion to him—she'd actually been fool enough to believe he'd wanted her to be his wife—she'd taken her baby-sitting savings and gotten a tiny butterfly tattooed on her bottom as a surprise for graduation.

Graduation night, instead of being pleased, Brad had been horrified. "Nice girls," he'd said in disgust, "don't do such things." Then he'd unceremoniously dumped her.

He'd gone on to college where he'd majored in pinning butterflies and pretty sorority girls. The last she'd heard he'd married the daughter of his mother's best friend. She hoped he was happy with his proper wife.

No she didn't.

"Hey, sweetheart." Crew's voice broke into her thoughts. "Since you aren't doing anything . . . mind fixing me another one of those tall glasses of lemonade like you made me the other day? I'm near dying of thirst out here in the heat. I swear I don't think it's ever going to rain again."

"Yes, I mind," Alexia muttered into her hands. Raising her head, she glared over her shoulder at him. "You want lemonade, fix it yourself. You know where the kitchen is. I'm busy."

"Busy taking a nap . . ."

"I was *not* taking a nap!"

"Okay, daydreaming then."

"I was working," she vowed. "Now will you please go away so I can finish?" She turned her head away from Crew, dismissing him.

He didn't take the hint. "You working on my account?" he asked, strolling over from the doorway where he'd been lounging.

"No. I am not working on your account. I'm . . . I'm working on something else."

She could feel him standing just behind her chair, looking down over her shoulder.

"You're writing in invisible ink then I guess, huh?" he said dryly, observing the blank paper lying on her desk in front of her.

"Will you get the hell out of my bedroom?" she demanded, jumping up and pointing the way. She didn't have to explain to him that she was still having trouble coming up with an idea for the amusement park account. Especially not when he was the cause of her block.

"Okay, okay. . ." Crew held up his hand to stop the tirade he could sense was coming. Grinning unrepentantly, he said, "Let me guess. What you are is hot, sweaty, tired, embarrassed and furious. Well, maybe not hot and sweaty," he amended, taking in her cool stare. "But what you're not is amused, right?"

Alexia continued to glare at him. "That's right. I am *not* amused. So take your clever sweet-talk and your cute little behind out of here." *Oh, heavens, had she really said that?*

"Cute little behind? Really. . . ?" His amber eyes danced as he glanced over his shoulder at the topic of discussion.

"Go!" she ordered, her cheeks flaming.

"Aw, come on, Alexia. Don't be embarrassed. I don't mind if you fancy my...um...tush. You've got a right saucy one yourself, if you don't mind my saying so."

Alexia squeezed her eyes closed and clenched her fists. "Will you ple-ease get back to work!"

"Now don't be like that, sweetheart."

"I am *not* your sweetheart."

"You could remedy that if you played your cards right," Crew teased, seeming to enjoy adding fuel to her fire.

"Played my. . . Get out! This has all been a mistake. I should never have agreed to your. . . your barter arrangement. I should have known better. You haven't done anything to finish the fish pond. That hole in the yard you're supposed to be digging never gets any bigger. I don't believe you know how to build a fish pond.

"You lied to me. I want you to leave. I want you to get your stuff and just. . . just leave."

She was shaking when she finished her tirade and her eyes were blurred with tears of pent-up frustration.

"Aw, hell . . ." Crew swore, pulling her into his arms.

Alexia made a low sound when his lips slowly descended to hers. Her restless hunger flared to life and she slid her fingers into his dark hair inching up the intensity of his caress.

Embers of desire, long banked, flickered then flared with tantalizing promise, building a shimmering heat between their bodies.

Crew's marauding tongue tempted her, coaxing her to open her mouth to him while his hands drew her closer and closer still.

And then it was she who couldn't get close enough, she whose kisses were driven by urgent passion, she whose hips moved against him in a surge of wild abandon.

With a groan, Crew lifted her leg, wrapping it around his hip, wedging himself firmly against her.

Alexia bit and sucked the strong column of his throat, tasting his salty essence. She began to nibble his ear. Then, growing ever more daring, Alexia flicked her warm, moist tongue just inside his ear causing a tantalizingly erotic sensation.

Crew's shudder of arousal was instantaneous. He reacted with an oath, sliding his hand up the back of her exposed thigh. Caressing her smooth skin, he worked his way higher and then higher yet, until his long fingers had worked their way around to the tender flesh of her inner thigh.

She gasped softly when she felt his fingertips slip beneath the lace edge of her panties.

Their breathing was labored, their quick pants the only sound in the silent room. No radio played to interrupt with the reality of time and temperature... civilization didn't intrude.

What did intrude was the clatter of Alexia's glasses that were knocked to the floor when Crew leaned her back across her desk. Pulling away from him abruptly, she retrieved her glasses, but slipping them on did nothing to hide her flushed face.

"Do you still want me to leave?" Crew asked gently.

Alexia went to stand by the French doors beside her desk, her back to him, struggling to regain the control she'd so easily lost. "I want you to leave me alone," she lied.

"That wasn't the impression I got...."

"Just go," she demanded in a tone that brooked no argument.

"Right."

When she heard the back door close, Alexia continued standing at the French doors, engulfed by the sound of loneliness.

Dear Editor:

Crew and Alexia have reached yet another impasse. I've had it with these two. I really, really have. Now Alexia wants Crew to leave her alone. Great.

Listen, would it be all right with you if I *just took off with Crew for a while . . . he's getting* real *frustrated.*

Tiffany

8

"I THINK SHE LIKES ME," Crew said, grinning widely and feeling the afterglow of a runner's high as he sat sprawled on the sofa after his early-morning run. "What do you think, Sam?" he asked, tugging Sam's kerchief.

Sam pricked up his ears and whined.

"Shut up, Sam. What do you know. You can't even remember not to chew holes in my running shoes." Crew eyed the beat-up athletic shoes he was wearing. One was white and the other navy blue. Sam was like the clothes dryer at the laundromat; he never ate things in pairs.

"I know Alexia needs me," Crew continued, doffing his damp T-shirt and mismatched shoes.

Sam pretended to be listening, cocking his head from side to side, but Crew knew he was more interested in the half-eaten Snickers candy bar lying on the coffee table in front of the sofa. Crew ate frozen Snickers for breakfast and had yet to finish one; Sam always managed to steal them first.

Crew rubbed his wadded T-shirt across his sweaty chest, continuing to think out loud. "She doesn't have a clue, you know, that Colby Langston is up to something. What I've got to do is figure out a way to make her see him for the polished pretender he is." He hoped he would be more successful at protecting Alexia from Colby than he'd been at protecting his mother from the oily sort that had eventually become his stepfather.

He had to admit his mother had been happy enough. She hadn't seen the man's obvious flaws, or maybe she hadn't wanted to. Was Alexia like that, too? he wondered. Maybe she, like his mother, would choose a pretender given the choice.

No matter, he had to try to make her see.

Crew had to admit that his efforts weren't completely altruistic. But it had been such a long time since he'd been in touch with his feelings, that he wasn't sure it was love he was falling into. A loner, he was self-reliant and had a wry perspective on the world, but in his relationships he'd been emotionally absent.

"Well, I've got to shower and get to work, pal. Try and have the place cleaned up by the time I get home and I'll take you along to Alexia's again," Crew said, looking around and shaking his head at the organized chaos of the trailer. "I hate Mondays," he groaned, forcing himself up from the comfort of the sofa and heading for the shower and another hot day on the scaffolding. If he'd thought it would have done any good, he'd have done a rain dance. The summer was turning into one hell of a drought.

MONDAY NIGHT Crew kept his distance, leaving Alexia alone as she'd requested. Sitting at her desk in her bedroom trying to work, Alexia heard him pull up in his truck and then several hours later heard him leave.

She'd steeled her resolve and hadn't once gone to the kitchen window to watch him.

Crew Harper wasn't what she wanted, she had to keep reminding herself...or rather he wasn't the life she wanted for herself.

She wanted a professional man and the life-style that entailed, guaranteeing any children she might have would grow up without experiencing the poverty she'd had to endure. A grueling, grinding poverty that had savaged her self-confidence and almost claimed her soul. She would have withered inside if it hadn't been for the free library books she'd escaped into.

No, Crew Harper with his devil-may-care attitude was not the man for her, no matter what her body kept insisting. She was sure she'd meet the kind of man she wanted within Colby Langston's circle.

In the meantime, she had her work.

Work that wasn't going at all well, she sighed, looking down at the blank paper before her.

The rest of the week crawled by. At first Alexia forbade herself to look out the window to where Crew was working when she found herself in the kitchen. Her resolve lasted only one night. Then she took to looking out the window when she went to the kitchen, but only for brief moments. When Sam had barked at a squirrel scrambling up a tree, Crew had looked up and almost caught her watching him at one such moment.

Thursday evening Alexia lingered at the kitchen window long enough to see Crew bring a cooler so he wouldn't have to come into her house at all. As she stood there, she noted he was getting tanner . . . that he needed a haircut . . . and that Sam would occasionally drop a yellow tennis ball at Crew's feet trying to coax him to play with him.

On Friday, Alexia stood at her window trying to come up with a good rationalization, one she could make herself believe, for why she should go out and help Crew with the fish pond. The hole in her backyard had grown steadily larger, despite the lack of rain that made the ground condition less than ideal for digging.

"This is getting crazy. If I don't think of some way to protect myself from Crew Harper's sensual pull, I'm going to wake up with him in my bed one of these mornings," she mumbled to herself. "What I need is a string of garlic or something," she said, half laughing at her fanciful thought. It was too late for garlic anyway as Crew had already bitten her on the neck in the Tunnel of Love. . . .

But she did need some way to protect herself, she thought, looking at Crew silhouetted in the gathering dusk. Some way to keep him out of her bed. . . some way to protect herself from herself. . . "But that's it!" she said out loud with a snap of her fingers, heading for the rose garden.

Saturday morning found Alexia Grant smiling. Not only had she carried out her idea of the night before, but she'd also come up with an idea for the amusement park as well. She'd gotten it while sitting up in bed with a carton of ice cream punching a spoon in and out of the frozen dessert, alternately licking off the spoon and trying to come up with the idea that had finally come to her in a dream. A rather erotic dream . . .

It was late, a little after midnight. She was propped up in bed against a mound of soft ruffled pillows, wearing nothing more than a pair of apricot bikini panties. The tea-cozy mystery she was trying to read wasn't getting rid of her craving for Swiss chocolate almond ice cream as she'd hoped it would.

She looked at the clock again. Once more she returned her attention to the book in her hand, trying to concentrate on the cast of characters who were suspects in the English country manor. It didn't work. She had to get up and go to the store for the ice cream she was craving.

Annoyed at her lack of self-control, she promised herself she would do extra laps at the gym as atonement for giving in. Since the supermarket was open all night and not far, she didn't bother to get redressed, pulling on a lightweight cotton wrap instead. After slipping on a pair of sandals, she headed out into the darkness to satisfy her craving.

The grocery store was doing a pretty good business despite the time, and she began to doubt the wisdom of coming out as she had. She felt uncomfortable in the brightly lit store, knowing what she didn't have on beneath her wrap. But deciding that as long as she was already there, she might as well pick up the ice cream, she headed for the frozen-food section. After all, only she knew she was half-dressed.

She picked up a carton of Swiss chocolate almond ice cream and was on her way to the checkout when she saw Crew Harper just ahead of her. He had a boxed cake in one hand, a bottle of champagne in the other. "Would you write Happy Birthday on this please?" he asked the bakery clerk who took the chocolate cake from him.

Turning to glance around the store while he waited, Crew spied her. "Alexia! What on earth are you doing here at this time of night?"

She was trapped.

"I couldn't sleep . . . ah, I was working on the amusement park account," she explained, not wanting him to think he was the cause of her not being able to sleep. She shrugged. "Then I got this craving for ice cream . . ."

"Here you are, sir," the bakery clerk interrupted, handing Crew his cake. Crew took the cake and turned back to Alexia. "Listen, this is great. I've got cake and champagne and you've got ice cream. You have to celebrate with me."

"I don't know . . ." Why hadn't she gotten dressed.

"Aw come on, Alexia, please . . ." he coaxed as they walked to the cashier.

"I suppose we could go back to my house," she suggested. Once home, she could excuse herself and get dressed properly.

When they got outside, Crew followed her to her car. "You know, I've got a better idea," he said. "Let's just eat here in your car. I'm starved. It will be like a birthday picnic."

Alexia swallowed dryly. "In my car...here...now...?"

"Right. But let's take the back seat so we can be comfortable. There's no room to set this stuff on those bucket seats in the front."

"I don't know..." Alexia hesitated.

"Humor me, it's my birthday, remember."

"You're sure. It really is your birthday?"

Crew nodded and ushered her into the back seat, then joined her. He snapped his fingers. "I forgot to get candles. How am I going to make a birthday wish? I know, I'll pick a number from one to ten and you have to guess it," he suggested.

"Six," she chose, deciding to humor him. The sooner they ate the cake and ice cream, the sooner she could leave.

Crew chuckled. "Wrong. Now you have to sit on my lap."

"What?"

"That was my birthday wish."

"I'm *not* sitting on your lap. You can just forget it."

"But, it's my birthday wish. You have to honor it. I don't bite, you know. Come on, Alexia. It will be easier for you to give me my birthday kiss that way."

"Birthday kiss . . . ?"

"You are going to give me my birthday kiss, aren't you?"

Crew sounded so woebegone that Alexia decided to humor him to move things along. What could one little birthday kiss hurt?

It was tight maneuvering, but she wound up on his lap, her lips pursed to bestow him with a quick chaste kiss.

"No, not yet. First we have to eat the cake and ice cream," Crew insisted, handing her his penknife to cut the cake.

She was ready to scream. If she was conscious of her half-dressed state before, sitting on Crew's lap brought it home with hot intensity. It was dark in the parking lot and dark in the car. Only the moonlight guided her cutting the cake. "Umm . . . this is great," Crew said, taking a bite of the moist, chocolatey cake she cut him. "Here, taste," he said, wiping a swipe of icing off the top of his piece with his forefinger and slipping his finger into her mouth.

There was nothing for her to do but suck the chocolate icing off while she squirmed inside, wanting to cross her legs and not daring to.

Crew popped the champagne, offering it to her before he took a swig. "Aren't you having any cake?" he asked.

"No, I want ice cream . . . but I don't have anything to eat it with."

"Don't be such a priss. Use your fingers."

Removing the lid from the carton, she found herself doing just that, sighing with pleasure as she slid the cold, rich dessert around in her mouth to savor it.

"Wow, what flavor is that?" Crew asked, his voice full of teasing laughter.

"Swiss chocolate almond," she informed him, the words garbled around the second mouthful of ice cream she'd just scooped up with her fingers.

"I've definitely got to try it." Shifting his weight, he settled her more intimately on his lap. "Now about my birthday present," he began.

"But I don't have a present for you. I didn't know it was your birthday."

"I didn't want you to buy me something. Bought presents are no big deal. I like presents where you give of yourself," he said, running his fingers on the inside of the collar of her wrap. Time seemed to stand still as he slowly began loosening the top of her wrap. "I've got a great idea. . . . Why don't we combine my birthday kiss with my birthday present."

"What . . . no . . . wait . . ." she said, pulling away.

He nuzzled her ear, his whispered words sending delicious shivers up her spine. "Relax, I only want to see you, that's all. I can tell you're not wearing a bra. Let me see how beautiful you are. . . ."

The sensual pull of his coaxing words relaxed her resistance and she allowed him to continue opening the top of her wrap, thinking these overt displays of affection—or O.D.A.s as he called them—were getting out of hand. But the pleasure of his fingers on her made her cease to care.

"You're beautiful. . . ." Crew said in hushed awe.

She wanted him to touch her, kiss her. "Your...birthday kiss..." she murmured, her voice laced with a yearning desire.

As she watched heavy lidded, Crew scooped up a dollop of ice cream from the carton to his mouth. A heartbeat later he lowered his mouth to her pebbled nipple...cold and heat closing on it. She crossed her legs and shuddered, a moan of pleasure escaping her lips as hot spasms of pleasure arrowed through her...

And then she'd awoken from the dream to find herself sitting upright in bed wearing nothing but a pair of apricot panties...a carton of Swiss chocolate almond ice cream at her side, a spoon in her hand.

Looking down, she saw the melting dollop of ice cream that had slid from her spoon to her breast when she'd dozed off. Using her forefinger, she lifted the melting ice cream from her breast to her mouth, sucking the sweet coolness from her finger as she got up to carry the ice-cream carton and spoon back to the kitchen.

She put the ice cream in the freezer section and leaned against the refrigerator and smiled. Crew Harper was plain old fun . . . even in a naughty dream. It was then she realized she had the idea for the amusement park that had been eluding her. The Funland Amusement Park should have a name that reminded her of the kind of good time a man like Crew could show her. She'd call the park Cheap Thrills. . . .

IT WAS BEGINNING to cloud up late Saturday afternoon as Alexia put the finishing touches to her presentation for the amusement park account.

Most of the major theme parks were expensive packages and very structured, requiring almost no input from the customer. Going to Funland with Crew had shown her it was more fun to participate and share the experience.

Her plan was to change the name of the amusement park from Funland to the Cheap Thrills Amusement Park . . . offering old-fashioned entertainment at good old-fashioned prices. With lower prices customers would go to the amusement park more often as a means of celebrating everything from getting a new job to, well . . . birthdays.

There was a knock at her bedroom door and Alexia turned to see Crew standing there, Sam lying at his feet. Crew looked tired from a day of shoveling the hard ground, but the stubble on the planes of his jaw made him dangerously handsome.

"You look like you could use a nap," Alexia said.

He glanced at the mosquito netting draping her bed. "A nap would be nice. . . ."

"I'm going out tonight, so why don't you go on home early," she suggested, ignoring his invitation.

A gust of wind blew a sprinkle of light rain against the panes of her French doors. Crew smiled sardonically. "Now it rains."

Alexia looked puzzled at his comment.

"I just came in to let you know I've finished digging the hole for the pond and it's ready for the plastic liner," he explained.

"Oh."

"So maybe tomorrow if you have time, I thought you could give me a hand spreading old newspapers before placing the tetra liner over it."

"Sure," Alexia agreed.

There was silence between them for a moment as Crew studied her. Finally he spoke. "So, you're going out tonight, huh?"

Alexia nodded.

"With Buttercup?" Crew asked, leaning against the door frame and crossing his ankles.

"With Colby Langston, yes," she corrected with thinly veiled impatience.

"Where are you going?" he asked, studying his fingernails a little too casually.

"Out," she answered avoiding his question.

"That's a good sign. But where exactly out?"

"To the Art Museum," she answered with some reluctance, remembering all too well how Crew had shown up at Wolff's and taken over the evening.

"Ah . . . going to the opening gala for the Pop Art retrospective, then?"

"You know about it?" she asked, not managing to keep the surprise from her voice.

"I guess opening galas are more your speed than say. . . amusement parks, huh?"

She just stared at him.

He nodded. "So, I don't suppose there's any chance I could just stick around and watch you get all gussied up for the gala, is there?" he asked, scratching his stubbled chin with his thumb, his amber eyes twinkling with unspoken promise.

She continued to stare at him, refusing to respond to his game.

"I didn't think so," he said with a shrug of his wide shoulders as he pushed away from the door frame and entered her bedroom.

Her eyes widened. Now what was he up to, she wondered, watching him through narrowed eyes.

He crossed over to her closet and pushed back the bifold doors. Glancing over the contents he asked, "So, what are you planning on wearing?" He began flipping through the rack.

"Will you stop that? What are you doing? I don't believe you."

"Why? I'm just trying to be helpful," he said, a grin playing around his lips as he selected a high-necked, long-sleeved gold lame dress. "I think you should wear this," he said, holding it up for her inspection.

Alexia closed her eyes, then opened them. "I'm not wearing that, now will you please put it back."

"Why not? It's a nice dress . . . it . . . it covers . . . it's a nice dress."

"It's a holiday dress, okay? I'm not wearing it."

Crew held up his hand good-naturedly. "Whatever you say. Wear what you like . . ." he paused in mid-thought, his attention caught by something in her closet. Reaching in he pulled out a black strapless number with a slit that would reveal a flash of leg.

Crew whistled appreciatively. "Correction. Wear whatever you want except this."

"What's wrong with that?" she demanded, having paid way too much for it when she'd bought it on impulse.

Crew's answering grin was palpitatingly wicked. "Absolutely nothing. But you're not to wear it unless you're with me, understand."

"Give me that," Alexia said, having had enough. She sprang from her chair, took the dress from him and put it back in her closet.

"I'll see you tomorrow," she said, looking pointedly at the door.

"Remember, don't stay out too late. I want to get an early start and I'll need your help." He walked halfway to the door then turned around. "Listen, Sam and I were thinking about getting some burgers and cheese fries. Then he's been wanting me to rent that video, *K-9*, cause it has a dog in it that looks like him. After that I thought maybe I might bowl a couple of games . . . You wouldn't want to cancel out on Buttercup and the gala and join us, now would you?"

"Tempting as that all sounds . . ." she said, trying to keep from smiling, "I don't break dates."

Crew nodded. "Then it is a date . . ."

Alexia just stared at him.

"Right. Well, come on, Sam, I guess it's just you and me," Crew said, turning and heading for the door.

"Crew?"

He turned.

"It's not your birthday today, is it?"

"No. Why do you ask?"

Alexia shrugged. "Nothing. I just wondered, that's all."

Dear Editor:

Yes, yes. I do understand about publishers having very strict rules about authors fraternizing with their characters. If you'll excuse me now, I'm going out for a carton of Swiss chocolate almond ice cream . . .

Tiffany

P.S. Could you hurry my cheque? I just saw this black strapless dress with a slit . . .

9

"I'M GLAD YOU FINALLY came up with a concept for the amusement park," Colby said holding the large black umbrella over Alexia with one hand while he straightened the shawl collar of his tuxedo with the other.

Taking Alexia's elbow, he assisted her in climbing the flight of steps to the Art Museum entrance. "You'll have to show me your presentation when I take you home."

Alexia nodded. She could feel her hair going wild and curly from the weather. "I'm really pleased with how the presentation turned out. I was beginning to think I was never going to come up with an idea."

"How *did* you get the idea?" Colby asked, closing the umbrella and handing it an attendant as they entered the museum.

Alexia felt a flush creep up her neck. "Ah... Oh, look! Why it's like a fairyland in here."

The Sculpture Hall had indeed been transformed for the opening night party. Tables for ten were covered with gold and silver cloths. The chairs at the tables were gold and had been flown in from Chicago for the event. In the center of each table was a huge crystal bowl containing masses of silver sprays hung with gold stars. At each place was a china setting set off by gold flatware.

"Yes, it's always quite nice," Colby said, having grown used to such lavish displays.

Alexia was glad she'd called Colby to tell him about finishing the amusement park presentation. It had been during the call that Colby had remembered he had an extra ticket for the gala and suggested she attend with him, saying it would be good for her to mingle with the movers and shakers of the city.

It wasn't a date as she'd allowed Crew to think. It was merely business, though she found it hard to think of business in such a magical setting. The large space was scented with the flowers that floated in and banked the fountains. She could hear the strains of a jazz quartet, but she could barely see the musicians in the crush of people. Alexia wondered what Crew would think of all the glitter and glamour surrounding her, the men in tuxedos, the women in gowns and jewels.

"See that tall, rather distinguished-looking man over there?" Colby asked, taking Alexia's elbow and guiding her a few feet to her left for a better view.

Alexia nodded.

"He's the curator of Twentieth Century Art and the man he's speaking with is one of the artists," Colby informed her. "The artists flew in for the installation. Tell you what, why don't I get us some champagne and then we'll try to work our way over to them. Wait here and I'll be right back."

Colby began working his way through the throng of people by the bar, and when he reached it, he was joined by the Challis brothers.

"Colby," Eric Challis said, clapping him on the back. "Haven't seen much of you at the polo matches lately, but now I understand why."

Colby followed Eric's glance to Alexia.

"Tell me," Eric continued, "how did a guy who got thrown out of half the prep schools in town for cheating happen to wind up with the prettiest woman in the room?"

"You got thrown out with me," Colby said defensively.

"Yeah, and I'm here with my brother. What's the scoop on the little fox over there? Is she your private stock or fair game for poaching?"

Colby shrugged. "She's a little nobody. Works at the Gund & Associates advertising firm where I do, only she actually works."

Eric jabbed Colby in the ribs conspiratorially, "Still talking gullible sweet young things into doing your work for you, eh?"

"Hush," Colby said with wink. "This one's so gullible, she doesn't know she's doing it."

"Uh-oh, looks like someone just sniffed out your fox," Eric's younger brother, Derrick, observed, nodding to where Alexia was waiting in the crowd.

"What's *he* doing here?" Colby asked, his eyes narrowing as he watched Crew Harper approach Alexia.

Alexia sensed Crew's presence behind her even before he leaned over her shoulder and whispered his admonishment in her ear.

"I thought I told you not to wear that dress."

Alexia swung around to confirm her suspicion. Crew Harper indeed stood before her, resplendent in a contemporary-cut black tuxedo with wide satin lapels. The white wing-tip tuxedo shirt he wore set off his tan. Where one would have expected a matching satin bow tie at his neck, Crew wore his black bolo tie with the silver steer head catch. Five o'clock shadow ghosted his jaw. He was drop dead to die for sexy.

"What . . . what are you doing here?" she demanded in a hoarse whisper, sounding as if the cops were looking for him.

His amber eyes twinkled as he grinned down at her from the added height a pair of black snakeskin cowboy boots lent him. "Like I keep telling you, everybody's got to be somewhere."

"You . . . you . . . that's why you wanted to know where I was going tonight. You followed us and snuck in somehow. If I were you, I'd leave before someone finds out and tosses your . . . tosses you out."

"I beg your pardon. I did not sneak in . . . not that I couldn't have if I'd wanted to."

"Then how did you get in? Are you here with someone?" she asked, looking around to see who might have brought him.

"I got in the hard way. I shelled out a hundred and fifty bucks for a ticket. Not like ol' Buttercup who probably got his tickets from Daddy, right? Where is he anyway?"

"He's at the bar getting us some champagne . . . Why are you here?"

"I wanted to see the art, of course. Isn't that why you're here?" When she didn't answer right away, he said, "Don't disappoint me and tell me you're here for the same reason as half the people in this room . . . only to see and be seen."

Alexia opened her mouth and then closed it again in frustration. Imagine Crew Harper chastising her for her values. And the worst of it was that he was right.

"Have you been to look at the paintings yet?" he asked finally, letting her off the hook.

"No, but . . ."

"Neither have I. I just got here. I had to go to three video stores before I could find Sam his *K-9* video," he said with a wink.

Crew took her hand, his rough calluses at odds with his suave attire. The contrast sent shivers of delight through her.

"Come see them with me. Buttercup'll catch up."

"I don't think—"

"That's right, don't think," Crew said, leading her through the crowd to a connecting hallway.

"Are you sure you know where you're going?" Alexia asked, trailing after him. They'd traveled several yards down the hall and hadn't met anyone in passing.

"This'll do," he whispered, pulling her off into a shadowy alcove.

"Just what do you think you're doing?" she demanded when he pinned her against the wall.

"I told you not to wear that dress," he murmured, nuzzling her neck.

"I'll wear whatever I want!" she replied adamantly, twisting in his embrace.

"Then you must be prepared for me to take my retribution..." Lifting his head, he stared down at her, his eyes flashing with mischief. "Let's see, what shall it be?"

"Will you quit! You're mad..."

"Well, that dress is designed to drive a man insane. Or rather you are, the way you look poured into it." Still considering her fate, he asked, "Shall I take a kiss for your penance?"

She lifted her chin and turned her face away from him, her expression telling him not to dare.

He chuckled, then growled, "No, I think not. It would muss your lipstick and people would know. I want this to be our little secret. Besides, if I kissed you like I want to kiss you..." He let the imagery hang in the air between them, sultry and provocative.

After a few moments he took her chin with his thumb and forefinger and turned her to face him. "What then? Any suggestions?"

She just stared at him.

"Hmm... and I thought you were the creative type, being in advertising and all. No ideas, huh?" he taunted.

She continued to stare at him in silence.

"I know," he said, glancing at the small window next to the alcove, its panes spattered with rain. "I'll take a rain check and exact my retribution... later."

Taking the white carnation from his satin lapel, he swirled it between his fingers while studying her. Holding her eyes with his, he trailed the petals of the carnation along the side of her face, over her lips and ever so slowly down her neck. "I want you to remember every inch of skin this flower trails over," Crew whispered huskily.

She looked faintly puzzled, her eyes burning bright as if with fever.

"My lips will travel the same path when I exact my retribution. . . ." he promised, moving the carnation with exquisite dalliance across her bare shoulder. Toying with her amorously, he continued trailing the flower down the sensitive underside of her bare arm.

The pulse at her throat leaped when he smoothed the carnation languorously back up from her wrist, past the inside of her elbow to the top of the strapless dress.

She swallowed dryly as he skimmed the soft flower over the creamy swells of her breasts spilling over the top of her dangerously sexy black dress.

"I don't think I should let you off scot-free tonight, though, do you?" he dared.

She didn't react to his challenge, just watched him warily, her face flushed.

"Hmmm . . ." Moving in closer, Crew trailed his finger over her breast in a scorching path of heat, then on impulse, slipped it free of the gown's restraint.

Alexia gasped at his sudden action, the sound erotic in the quiet alcove.

Crew held her eyes with his own heavy-lidded ones as he covered her soft, plump nipple with the petals of the carnation, then twirled the flower around it. Her nipple pebbled instantly and sent incredible sensations of heat streaming directly to her groin.

He pulled the flower away when it had gotten the sensual effect he'd elicited, and he slipped her gown back in place, covering her. His grin was as sexy as sin as he rubbed the flower back and forth over his jaw, feeling her acquiescence to his seduction at that moment.

"Later..." he whispered, slipping the white carnation into her lush cleavage. "The flower is to remind you I hold your I.O.U." he said with a wicked wink.

"Are you quite finished?" she said, finding her voice.

"For now," he said agreeably. "Why don't we go have a look at the paintings." Taking her hand, he led her back to the Special Exhibition Gallery off the Sculpture Hall.

The paintings were installed on putty-gray backgrounds to complement the primary colors used on many of the canvases. The painting they stood before looked to Alexia like a blown-up panel of a comic strip, the centerpiece a huge teardrop.

"Neat, huh?" Crew said, still continuing to hold her hand.

"So here's where you've gotten off to," Colby called, coming to join them. "Sorry, Alexia, but they don't allow champagne in here," he apologized for coming back to her empty-handed.

"Shopping for Mr. Michael again?" Colby asked by way of greeting Crew.

"No. Just a fan of pop art," he said, continuing to admire the painting while allowing Alexia to slip her hand free of his.

"Yes, well . . . of course," Colby muttered, then turning to Alexia, he said, "There's someone I think you should meet. Why don't we come back here later and look at these. Nice seeing you again. What was the name . . . Harper?"

Crew gave Buttercup an amused nod, then turned his attention back to the paintings.

As she joined Colby, Alexia tried not to look down at the white carnation resting in her cleavage like a ticking time bomb.

"If I didn't know better I'd think that guy was following me around," Colby said, leading her back to the Sculpture Hall. Glancing down, he noted the carnation resting in her cleavage. "It's *you* he's following around, isn't it? What's going on between the two of you? I thought I warned you about seeing him socially. You know he's not exactly Gund & Associates style."

"Nothing is going on between us," she vowed. "He's building a fish pond for me in exchange for my doing an advertising layout for him. He's a client, nothing more. Got that? Crew Harper is just a client."

"Sure. I'm convinced."

Then why wasn't she? The question continued to haunt her for the rest of the evening.

ALEXIA STOOD at the kitchen counter in an oversize violet T-shirt eating Swiss chocolate almond ice cream directly from the carton with a spoon. Looking out the window over the sink, she saw that the rain had stopped and the sky had begun to clear. Here and there a bright star twinkled in the inky darkness.

It was after one o'clock and Colby had been gone for about an hour. He'd stayed longer than she'd expected, expressing an interest in every little detail of her presentation for the Funland Amusement Park account. When she'd finished showing it to him, he'd seemed really impressed with the job she'd done.

So despite the fact that she half expected Crew to show up at any minute to collect on his ridiculous I.O.U.—the white carnation was in a bud vase on her dressing table—she was feeling in really good spirits.

Maybe tomorrow afternoon when she and Crew were done lining the pond with newspapers and liners, she'd go back to the museum and have a look at the paintings. She hadn't gotten a chance to see them, as Colby had kept her busy meeting people.

She'd caught the occasional glimpse of Crew, and there was always some attractive woman at his side. Each time she'd seen him it had been someone different. The last one she'd seen him with had been a petite brunette in a bright red dress.

Crew Harper had something money couldn't buy.

But she wasn't going to think about Crew Harper.

She was going to think about how great it was going to feel to be a partner in Gund & Associates, now that Colby had convinced her that the sale to the Cheap Thrills Amusement Park was a sure bet. How had he put it? Oh, yes. "The owner is going to snap this up the minute he hears it."

She smiled.

As one of her favorite ads said, "You've Come A Long Way, Baby."

The little girl in hand-me-downs was receding farther and farther back into her memory.

ALEXIA PUT a Melissa Etheridge C.D. on to play, turning up the volume so she could hear it in the kitchen and because Melissa was one of those singers who sounded better played loud.

Crew had said he wanted to get an early start lining the fish pond, so Alexia had decided to surprise him. A half hour earlier she'd gotten back from The Eggery with take-out sausage and egg omelets and biscuits and gravy. After all, she did owe him for the warm chocolate croissants he'd shown up on her doorstep with one morning. And perhaps if she was lucky, he'd consider the breakfast as payment of his ridiculous I.O.U.

Looking at the clock, she saw it was after nine. He should have already arrived. Setting the oven on low, she placed the food she'd bought inside to keep it warm, while a container of fresh fruit she'd cut up chilled in the refrigerator awaiting his arrival.

So where was he?

Having breakfast in bed with the brunette in the red dress, her insecurity said, taking voice.

Shut up, she told herself.

Trying to keep her mind off the niggling thought, she began setting the table. That done, she went outside to her garden to cut a bouquet of flowers to put in a vase for a centerpiece.

A half hour later, Crew still hadn't arrived.

Where was he?

He's probably showering with the petite blonde in the pink silk jumpsuit—you remember the one with the Scarlett O'Hara wasp waist, her insecurity taunted.

Shut up, she told herself once again.

Looking in the oven to check on the food, she saw it was beginning to dry out, so she covered it with foil in the hopes that it would hold a while longer.

She poured herself a glass of orange juice and paced.

Where was he?

Probably with the brunette *and* the petite blonde, her insecurity conjured.

Yes, probably, Alexia agreed with herself.

Having lost her appetite, Alexia followed suit with her temper and turned off the oven and Melissa's tuneful outpouring of pain and unrequited love.

Crew Harper wasn't to be taken seriously, she knew that. Knew he played with women, charmed them, kissed them, probably even went to bed with them, and it was all in fun. It wasn't even something a woman could get angry about, she reasoned, unreasonably.

From the first moment she'd met him, she'd recognized him for what he was—a charmer, a world-class flirt. It was she who was foolish for reading more into his attention than that.

And anyway, she reminded herself, Crew Harper wasn't the sort of man she had in mind for herself at all. What she really wanted was a man who took life more seriously. One who aspired to . . . to . . . more than cutting someone else's lawn. A man who thought a night on the town was something more than buying some burgers and going bowling!

So why was it that last night, when she'd been at the Art Museum surrounded by men who could offer her anything her heart desired, her heart had only desired the one man who didn't meet her expectations?

A man who couldn't give her all the things she'd never had, the material things, the prestige.

A man who was as wild, impulsive—and ordinary—as she was.

"WHERE WERE YOU this morning?" Alexia demanded when Crew finally arrived at ten o'clock that night.

"I slept in, why?"

"You said you wanted to get an early start lining the fish pond and that you needed my help, remember?"

Crew laughed, the corners of his eyes crinkling. "You're not serious," he said, flopping onto the sofa.

Alexia planted her hands on her hips indignantly. "Of course, I'm serious! I wasted an entire morning waiting for you and you never showed up." She didn't mention the breakfast, not wanting him to know just how big a fool she was.

"But, Alexia, it was pouring rain last night." He frowned. "Or were you so taken with Buttercup and his society set that you didn't notice? It didn't stop raining until shortly after midnight and it was a real frog strangler. I figured the hole I dug for the fish pond had to have at least an inch of water in it."

Alexia dropped down on the sofa. All the righteous anger that had built since the morning drained from her and her shoulders slumped.

"Well, didn't it?" Crew asked, stretching his arms over his head.

"I don't know," Alexia mumbled.

"You don't know . . ."

"I didn't look, okay? I never thought . . ." she said, looking away in embarrassment.

"Listen," Crew said, reaching to take her hand. "I'm sorry. I should have called you. I was occupied and . . ."

"I'll bet," Alexia muttered, pulling her hand from his as images of the petite blonde and brunette that had been at the gala flashed in her mind.

"What's *that* supposed to mean?" Crew demanded.

"Nothing." Trying to change the subject, she asked, "Where's Sam? I thought I saw him with you when you came in."

Crew glanced around the living room and shrugged. "He must have crawled off somewhere and gone to sleep. He cut his paw this morning on a glass I dropped and I had to take him to the vet."

"Is he okay?"

"Yeah, the vet gave him some pills to keep him sleepy so he'll stay off his paw pretty much, but he'll be fine."

Alexia nodded. So he'd spent the morning with Sam . . . not entertaining another woman as she'd imagined.

Standing, Crew said, "I brought some stacks of old newspaper to line the pond with. I'll unload them from the truck and then I'll collect Sam and we'll be off."

"Let me help you," Alexia said, getting up.

It took several trips by both of them to stack the old newspapers by the pond.

"That's the last of them," Crew said, straightening, wiping his wrist across his damp forehead. The heat and humidity had shot up after the rain had ended, making the atmosphere closer than ever. "With this heat, the rest of the standing water should be gone by tomorrow evening. There might be some mud, but I think we should be able to lay the newspaper over it."

"Okay," Alexia said, pushing her hair back from her face. "I'll try to get home early tomorrow evening so I can help before it gets dark."

"I'll see you tomorrow then," Crew agreed as they headed back to the house. "Just let me collect Sam and we'll be out of here."

Opening the kitchen door a crack, Crew leaned in and yelled for the dog, "S-a-a-m."

Sam didn't come running as he usually did.

Crew frowned. "He must be really out of it from the pills the vet gave him. I'd better go find him."

Alexia followed Crew inside where a quick search of the house turned up Sam in her bedroom. He'd crawled under the mosquito netting and lay curled up in a ball, fast asleep in the center of Alexia's bed.

"Sam, come on, boy," Crew coaxed from the doorway as Alexia looked over his shoulder. "Quit playing possum now. It's time to go home."

Sam didn't come.

A worried frown creased Crew's brow as he strode over to the bed to check on the dog with Alexia close on his heels.

"Sam?" On closer inspection Crew saw that the dog was just sleeping deeply and the worried frown on his brow relaxed.

Leaning down to pick up the dog, Crew said, "I'll just carry him to the truck without . . . Ahhh-choo! . . . waking him."

When he rose with Sam in his arms, Crew also caught the end of the coverlet and top sheet covering Alexia's bed, pulling them with him.

"Ah-choo! Ah-ah-choo! Ach-choo!" Crew broke into such a sneezing fit he almost dropped Sam.

"What on earth . . . ?" Crew wondered out loud, glancing quickly around the room for a vase of roses. Seeing none, he turned to Alexia and asked, "Did you just put on some perfume with a heavy rose scent?"

She shook her head, a guilty flush creeping up her neck.

"Then you must have . . . ah-choo! . . . sprayed some sort of room freshener or something recently, right?"

Alexia was about to cop a plea when Sam woke up and struggled free of Crew's arms to jump back on Alexia's bed.

"Sam, we've got to go . . . ahhh-choo! . . . home . . ." Crew stopped in midsentence when he saw what he'd uncovered by trailing Alexia's coverlet and top sheet from the bed with Sam. Someone had sprinkled hundreds of rose petals on the bottom sheet.

He swung around to face Alexia. "Have you always slept on rose petals, sweetheart . . . or is this a recent habit since you found out I'm allergic to roses?"

The look on her face told him his answer.

"Lady, you got a problem and I ain't it."

CREW ARRIVED BACK at the trailer with Sam and carried him inside, laying him on the couch in front of the television. Flipping on the set for company while he raided the icebox for some leftover pizza, he heard Robin Leach of *Lifestyles of the Rich and Famous* informing him that everyone was rich and he wasn't.

Taking the pizza from the microwave, Crew carried it to the couch to share with Sam, who was showing signs of life again. Sitting down before the TV, Crew found as much to be amused about as to be envious of on the popular show.

They were showing a sexy movie siren's bedroom containing a huge bed made of rustic whitewashed timber. Crew thought back to Alexia's bed of rose petals and laughed.

Handing Sam the last piece of pizza, Crew said, "What do you think about those rose petals, Sam? Have I been insulted or complimented . . . what'daya think?"

Sam barked three times in rapid succession, then whined.

"Shut up, Sam."

ALEXIA SPENT AN HOUR picking up all the rose petals in her bed. Crew must have thought she was a complete nitwit. One would think by now she'd have learned not to act on her impulses.

Tomorrow she was going to take off early and have all the newspapers already down before Crew even got there. That way she wouldn't have to see the laughter in his eyes.

CREW LAY IN BED listening to Sam snore at his feet.

Maybe he should take one of Sam's pills from the vet so he could sleep, he thought. Chuckling to himself, he decided it wasn't a good idea—he might wake up with a penchant for chasing cars and sniffing ladies . . . No, it wasn't a good idea.

Alexia Grant wasn't a good idea, either.

Oh sure, he was physically attracted to her. One hell of a lot. But when it came to actually liking her, he wasn't so sure. How could he like someone who practically worshiped Colby Langston and his set? While there was nothing wrong with having money, it sometimes corrupted weak people. People like Colby Langston and his idle bunch. What would Alexia think if he told her what he'd overheard at the Art Museum about Colby and Eric Challis?

When Alexia wasn't buying into the yuppie thing, he found her delightful, but clearly her values were mixed up. Sometimes he couldn't understand why he was even bothering to try to help her, especially when she was being snobby and didn't even realize it.

Or are you being a snob in reverse? his conscience asked. Was he criticizing her for trying because he was afraid to? Was he afraid to try because he might fail? Had he decided having something and then losing it was worse than never having it all? Had his father's death and mother's rejection crippled him? Was that why he never committed to anything?

As he drifted off to sleep, he thought maybe he would really try to make something of the landscaping business idea of his after all.

Dear Editor:

I have a feeling Crew is going to collect on his I.O.U. real soon . . .

Tiffany

10

IT HAD BEEN one hell of a Monday, but Alexia felt good as she'd managed to reschedule her three o'clock appointment so she could leave early to lay the newspapers in the fish pond before Crew arrived. She was just clearing her desk when Colby Langston arrived in her doorway with a prospective client in tow.

"Alexia, I'd like you to meet Eric Challis. He's thinking of hiring Gund & Associates to do some work for the Challis Foundation and I recommended you to him."

"But I . . ."

"I'd handle him myself, but I have a meeting I'm late for now."

"It's good to meet you, Miss Grant. Colby speaks very highly of you," Eric Challis said, stepping forward and offering his hand.

"Mr. Challis," Alexia acknowledged, pasting a smile on her face.

"Please call me Eric. . . ."

So much for getting away early.

IT WAS DARK by the time Alexia arrived home.

Eric Challis had invited her to join him for dinner, and as he was a potential client, it would have been awkward to refuse. He'd taken her to Anthony's, waltzing into one of the most expensive restaurants in town without a reservation. The owner had greeted him warmly by name and had then given them a choice table.

A menu never appeared, though black-coated waiters in abundance did, ringing their table like watchful penguins. Eric gave the head waiter a few suggestions and then while the waiter went to consult with the chef, the owner had come over to chat.

When the food came, their every wish was anticipated, though she didn't know how the waiters could see in the dark, hushed atmosphere. She'd almost felt as if she were in church.

Eating had seemed a deadly serious ritual, and while the food had been delicious—everything from the succulent prawns to the chocolate torte ladled with a tangy raspberry sauce—it had almost made her see the appeal of hamburgers and cheese fries.

She'd been impressed, she had to admit it. Eric Challis had succeeded in that. Everything about him had the quiet whisper of money, from his gold watch beneath his French cuffs to his imported car he'd insisted they take to the restaurant.

During dinner he'd mentioned a summer house and sailing, a family compound and polo matches. Eric's life-style was everything she aspired to even if he had inherited his position of privilege.

So why wasn't she thinking of Eric Challis now, instead of wondering why Crew Harper's truck wasn't in the driveway and whether Sam was all right.

It was hot and sticky when she got out of the air-conditioned car, but a frisky breeze was stirring the air, signaling a coming change.

She was almost at the front door of her house when she heard Crew's truck pull up.

"Where in the hell have you been?" he called, slamming the door of his truck, his legs eating up the distance to her.

"I was at work," she began, unlocking the door and going inside the house.

"No, you weren't. I was just there."

"What?"

"I got worried about you so I drove over to your office. Tell me, what was so all-fired important that you couldn't be here as we agreed or at least have telephoned?"

"I had a last-minute meeting with one of Colby's friends, Eric Challis," Alexia explained, taking off her suit jacket and slipping it over the back of the kitchen chair. The washed silk bodysuit she wore was torrid red and exactly matched the short, softly pleated skirt of her suit.

"A meeting... till ten o'clock at night?" A small muscle twitched in his square jaw, betraying the height of his fury.

Stepping out of her pumps, she walked in her stocking feet to the refrigerator for a glass of ice. "No, we went to dinner, too."

"Dinner was it? That's rich. I'm waiting here thinking something's happened to you and you're out playing footsie under some long, linen tablecloth with . . . Eric."

Alexia gave Crew a considering stare. He was way out of line, but he had a point. She closed her eyes and rubbed the bridge of her nose. "You're right. I should have called."

"Wrong. You should have been here. You don't go waltzing off to dinner when you've already made plans for the evening."

Alexia walked over to the sink, getting water from the tap. "I don't know what you're so upset about," she said, taking a drink. "It's not like we had a date or anything, you know."

Crew closed the space between them and took the glass of water from her hand, slamming it on the counter. With his face inches from hers, he glowered. "That's right. You don't have dates with me. I'm not good enough for you. You've made that more than clear. However, there's a summer storm threatening and that means more rain. A lot more. The newspapers and liner should have been laid tonight."

"Fine," she bit off, turning on her heel. Shoving open the kitchen door, she marched outside, letting the door slam behind her, punctuating her anger.

"Aren't you going to change your clothes at least?" he called after her. His words were lost on her. She was already on her way to the newspapers stacked beside the muddy hole in the backyard.

Uttering a curse, Crew slammed out the kitchen door. When his eyes adjusted to the dark, he saw the wind was dealing Alexia fits, lifting the newspapers as she struggled futilely to lay them down. Only one or two sheets of newspaper actually stuck in the mud; the rest had been lifted by the wind and scattered around the yard capriciously.

Yanking off his shoes and socks, Crew waded into the hole he'd dug for the fish pond, soft mud squishing between his toes.

"Will you stop!" he demanded, jamming his fists on his hips in exasperation when he reached her.

"No," she refused, her chin inching up stubbornly. "This has to be done tonight. You said so yourself. This is the only night in the whole year it can possibly be done."

"You're being . . ." Crew threw up his hands and his eyes beseeching the night sky.

"What? Ridiculous? Is that what I'm being? And what about you, Crew Harper—ranting and raving at me like you're some jealous husband. Well, I don't have a husband."

"Maybe you need one," he mocked, leaning in and invading her space.

"I hardly think so. I can take care of myself," she vowed, raising her hands to the solid wall of his chest to push him away from her.

Grabbing her wrists, Crew lost his footing in the slippery mud, falling back and pulling Alexia down with him in the wet, sticky mire.

Alexia squealed as they landed in a tangle with Crew sprawled on his back and Alexia on top of him.

He was grinning up at her, his lips mere inches from hers. "You can take care of yourself...*really?* Did I hear that right? And here I was under the distinct impression you were looking for some rich guy to take care of you. That was the whole point of your long dinner with Eric Challis tonight, wasn't it?"

"I told you that was business," she said, squirming to get off him.

"Careful, you don't want to damage anything you might want to use later," Crew chuckled as her knee grazed his groin.

"Ohh...!" Alexia sputtered, breaking one hand free. Reaching beside his head, she scooped up a handful of mud and aimed it as his grinning face.

Crew managed to twist his face away at the last minute and her aim missed its mark, landing with a plop beside his head.

"Why you little..." his narrow gaze impaled her and he shifted his lithe body, quickly pinning her beneath him.

"My turn," he said, his eyes dancing as he looked down at her.

Her lips parted and her breath came in shallow gasps as she looked up at him.

All of the sudden the laughter went out of his eyes to be replaced by a flare of sensual heat deep in their amber depths.

"Stop...stop looking at me that way," she whispered.

Dragging her eyes from his, she fastened her gaze on his inviting mouth. Slowly he lowered his lips to hers.

"No . . ." she whimpered, her eyes wide, pupils flaring as she twisted, her hands captured in his, pinned above her head in the mud.

"No . . . ?" he coaxed, his lips brushing hers, nipping at her full, pouty bottom lip.

And then all of a sudden they went out of control, going at each other, each slaking a desperate thirst...as though they'd been lost in a desert of unquenched desire for a lifetime.

His hand slipped to cup the back of her head, bringing her lips to his open mouth and probing tongue. His other hand slid up beneath her silky pleated skirt to ride along the inside of her smooth thigh slippery with mud. When Crew's hand squeezed at the juncture of her thighs, Alexia bowed toward him, moaning softly, her head thrown back as shudders of pleasure rocked her body.

"Lord help me, I want you." Crew's anguished whisper was hoarse and urgent in her ear as he fumbled with the buttons of her bodysuit, then unsnapped her lacy bra, freeing her lushness to his foraging mouth.

He groaned, pressing his hardness against her as his mouth closed over the soft mound of her breast while a light rain began to fall, enveloping them in a warm mist.

Alexia thrust her hands into his hair, urging him to take more of her into his mouth, the sucking sensation sending waves of hot desire to torment her aching femininity.

With an oath, Crew slid sideways into the warm mud, one hand bracing them as he pulled Alexia on top of him. As she straddled him, he reached up with his muddy hand and closed it over her breasts, smearing the warm mud over her in a satiny caress.

His mouth took hers again in an eating kiss as his hand stayed at her breast, twisting her nipple gently, but with enough pressure to build her growing need for him.

Leaning forward, Alexia pulled at Crew's T-shirt until she had it over his head. Discarding it, she applied handfuls of mud to the hard planes of his chest making sensual fingerpaints as she explored the cords of muscle and well-defined hollows.

"You're driving me out of my mind...." Crew groaned when she slipped her hand low on his abdomen. Stilling her hand, he pushed her top from her shoulders, pinning her arms while he ravished her neck with broad swaths of his tongue and nibbling kisses.

Finally he tugged her top down her arms until she was free of it. Sitting astride him, she was gloriously naked to the waist. The warm rain began falling harder, fat droplets plopping on the fullness of Alexia's upturned breasts then running in rivulets toward her belly.

She leaned forward, rubbing her rain-splashed breasts against the solid wall of his chest, which was slippery with mud. Her hardened nipples brushed his, eliciting a strangled groan from deep in his throat. She could feel his erection straining at the confinement of his jeans.

Bunching her soft-pleated skirt in a damp mass at her waist, his hands moved to massage and knead the swell of her cheeks while rubbing her up against his throbbing hardness. Alexia's breathing was ragged as she caught tiny gulps of air between hungry kisses.

Crew slowly inched his long fingers beneath the bottom of her bodysuit and made a thong of it so that his hands were smoothing her bare skin, the knowledge and sensation driving him wild as an image flashed in his mind.

"I can't . . ." He drew a long, shuddering breath. "I can't hold out much longer, Alexia," he swore, his hand moving to unsnap her bodysuit where it shielded her from his exploring hands.

When she was freed of the material's constraint, he cupped her, sliding two fingers inside her while he used the heel of his hand to grind small circles against her pubic bone. Alexia arching to his hand, begged, "Please, Crew . . ."

"Soon," he whispered hoarsely, his hand going to unsnap his jeans. "Just as soon as I get these off and kiss that pretty little butterfly on your sexy bottom."

Alexia went absolutely still in his arms.

"What did you say?" she asked, the chill in her voice stilling Crew's hand at midzipper.

He didn't answer her, knowing what he'd given away in the heat of passion.

Her voice trembled with hurt and fury. "It's dark. . . there's no way you could. . . and the mud. . . how could you possibly know . . . ?"

"I can explain," Crew said, reaching for her as she pulled away from him.

"And you will," she vowed, "but first I want a bath. I suddenly don't feel clean." Pushing herself up, she began sobbing and ran for the house.

Crew swore beneath his breath and went after her.

When he entered the house, he heard her bedroom door slam shut and then the sound of running water as she turned on the shower.

Crew walked back outside. The storm's building fury had finally unleashed a pounding rain that washed the mud from him and his jeans. As he walked back to collect his T-shirt, shoes and socks, he wished the rain would wash away the feeling of foreboding that enveloped him. The feeling that the fortune teller at the amusement park had been right; there was only going to be one love in his life. The physical attraction aside, he'd certainly never felt anything like what he felt for Alexia. She excited him, challenged him, delighted him . . . made him see the world in closer focus when he was with her. He was head over heels in love with her. Even Sam knew it.

And now he'd blown it.

When he went back inside, Alexia's bedroom door was still closed. Searching the kitchen drawers, he came up with a couple of terry-cloth dish towels to dry off his upper torso and feet, but his jeans remained sodden as he stood waiting to explain.

What could he possibly tell her? That he'd seen the tattoo when she'd removed her panty hose by the truck? No. The truth.

No smooth lines, no fancy footwork. If he loved her, he had to tell her the truth and take the consequences.

Her bedroom door opened.

Alexia came out wrapped in a thick white floor-length terry robe, her hair caught up turban style in a matching towel.

"I'm listening," she said, her eyes cold as she took a stool at the island counter.

Crew remained standing, leaning back against the sink, a terry dish towel slung over his bare shoulder.

"I work as a window washer. Your office building is one of my clients," he began.

"So that's where I've seen you before . . ."

"And where I saw you."

"I don't understand."

"I know. But I want you to understand that what happened was happenchance. It's not something I'm in the habit of doing," Crew said emphatically.

"Which is?"

"Ah . . ." Crew pulled the dish towel from his shoulder and wadded it into a ball, throwing it in the sink as he turned away from her. There was no way he could face her as he told her of his misdeed. Looking out the kitchen window that was streaked with rain, he picked his way over the land-mined subject. "You know how you sometimes change into your workout clothes in your office before you leave your building to go to the gym?"

"I know, but how do you know?"

"Well, a few weeks ago I watched you change," he said all in a rush to get the guilty admission out. He stood for a moment with his eyes squeezed closed, his teeth gritted, expecting her to explode or at the very least to find something whizzing by his head.

"You watched me?"

"Yes, through an opening in the drapery. You'd neglected to close it all the way. I was finishing up for the day at your window when I saw a movement inside your office from the corner of my eye. Since I was under the impression that most everyone in the building had cleared out for the day, I looked in and...well, you can imagine my surprise."

"That's when you saw my tattoo. You watched me undress."

Crew nodded, waiting for her words of censure and outrage. He was startled to hear instead the sound of her erupting laughter bubbling forth behind him. Not trusting what his ears were hearing, he swung around to face Alexia.

"You're not angry?" he asked in amazement when he saw that she was truly amused.

"It's just . . ." She went off in a series of giggles.

"What?" he demanded.

"Who would have thought to worry about a Peeping Tom on the fourth floor?" she said, grinning as she slipped off the stool and walked over to her bedroom door.

"I am *not* a Peeping Tom!"

Alexia looked over her shoulder, giving Crew back one of his wicked grins. "Shame," she said with a wink.

Crew blinked. It had all happened so quickly. She'd let her robe fall, he'd seen a quick flash of butterfly and then heard the click of the lock on her bedroom door.

He stood rubbing his hand across his bare chest as he stared at her bedroom door. Walking over to it, he knocked softly.

There was no answer.

Crouching, Crew put his eye to the keyhole.

It was dark, indicating she'd left the skeleton key in the lock. He grinned as he rose, an idea forming in his mind.

After a quick trip back outside to retrieve a dry newspaper and an old piece of wire from the truck, he returned to her locked bedroom door.

He knocked again. "Alexia . . ."

There was no answer.

Crouching down, he slipped the newspaper beneath her bedroom door, then inserted a piece of wire in the keyhole from his side until he worked the key on her side free and it fell to the newspaper he'd slipped under the door. Gingerly pulling the newspaper back to his side of the door, he was rewarded with the skeleton key. Picking it up, he unlocked her bedroom door.

"Is that right after knot tying in the Boy Scout manual?" Alexia asked when he entered.

She was sitting on her bed, once again wrapped in her robe, her legs crossed beneath her, her chin propped in her hands, thinking Crew Harper was audacious, delicious fun. Like her, he sometimes acted on impulse, but unlike her, he wasn't ashamed of his lower-class roots.

She was beginning to find she was happiest when she was with him. With him she could be the wild, impulsive and ordinary person she was. His only censure was of her materialistic values.

"No," Crew said, answering her question. "I learned it in my misspent youth."

"I'd like to hear about your misspent youth," Alexia said.

His hand rubbed his chest unconsciously as he countered with a wicked wink. "I'd rather *show* you some things I learned in my misspent youth."

"You surprise me," Alexia said. "I would have thought my tattoo would have offended you."

"You're kidding, right?" His hand stilled on his chest as he looked at her doubtfully.

"I got it to surprise the man I had planned to marry. He broke off with me when he saw it. He thought a woman having a tattoo was really cheap." She lowered her head. The hurt in her voice reflected how deeply she'd been affected by the rejection.

Crew shrugged. "Well, that's his problem, isn't it?"

Alexia unbowed her bent head. "I never thought of it that way," she said, looking up at him.

"Personally, I find your tattoo exciting."

"Really. . . ?"

He nodded. With slow strides he approached her bed, his eyes never wavering from hers. "So exciting, I'd like a closer look myself."

"You didn't get a close enough look the first time?" Alexia asked.

"Sweetheart, I've been wanting to get closer to you since the first time I saw you," he said, leaning into her and causing her to tumble backward beneath him on the bed.

"*Crew*...your pants are soaking wet from the rain," she objected.

"Okay, okay," he said, getting up with a chuckle. Reaching for his zipper, he said, "I'll simply take them off. And while I'm at it, I think I'll take a shower to get rid of any remaining mud. Want to join me?"

"I'm already clean," she answered, propping herself up on her elbows.

"I know. I was thinking more along the lines of getting dirty together in the shower."

"Go!"

"Yes, ma'am," he answered, heading for the shower. Stopping just outside the bathroom, he called over his shoulder, "Be sure and pencil me in your little black book for say... umm... the next several hours.

She threw a pillow at him.

Moments later Alexia heard the rush of running water and Crew's off-key rendition of "Blame it on the Rain." He really was incorrigible. Her sentiment was magnified tenfold, when a short while later, the shower stopped and he came strolling out of the bathroom with a towel slung low on his hips and her bottle of baby oil in his hand.

"Look what I found," he said with a wicked wink.

"It wasn't lost."

"Maybe not, but I'll bet it was wasted... until now."

"What do you mean?"

"Slip out of your robe and I'll show you," he said, unscrewing the cap on the bottle of baby oil.

"Give me that," Alexia demanded, reaching for the bottle.

"The robe, Alexia . . ." he insisted, holding the bottle just out of reach.

She made a lunge for the bottle, but he was quicker, evading her grasp.

"Aw, come on, Alexia. You were daring enough to get a tattoo on your tush from a stranger. You're not going to wimp out on me, are you? Surely you're game for a little massage."

She didn't undo the robe, but he could tell she was wavering. All she needed was a little nudge to capitulate. A gleam of mischief surfaced in his eyes, "I dare you . . ."

"Rat," she said, slipping out of the robe as he'd known she would, given a dare. "Where do you want me?" she asked.

"Just stay kneeling on the bed," he said huskily. "I'm going to warm the baby oil in the microwave and make you feel better than you've ever felt in your life, sweetheart."

She smiled. "Cocky, aren't we?"

He undid the towel at his hips, looked down, and as immodest as hell, nodded, his world-class flirty grin in place as he left for the kitchen.

He returned to her side moments later, baby oil in hand.

Kneeling face-to-face on the bed, their eyes locked in intense sensual awareness, he began. Pouring a dollop of warm oil on each breast, he set the bottle aside and began slicking his hands over their pert lushness.

Her breasts were satiny warm in his callused hands as he spread his fingers wide, tickling his palms, sliding them back and forth over her smooth nipples that had puckered into cool beads at his touch.

His eyes shuttered closed and he lowered his head, trailing his furled tongue between her breasts while his hands continued to squeeze and massage her slippery globes.

Lowering her back on the bed, he continued; his tongue moving down in a straight line to her navel. He reached for the baby oil again trickling it in the same damp path. Using the flat of his hands, he spread the oil outward and upward, then pleasured his palms again with the shape of her curved waist.

"Aw, the hell with this," he swore, pulling her into a deep embrace punctuated by an openmouthed, eating kiss that stoked the heat of their raging passion.

"Uh-uh..." Alexia objected practically breathless as she squirmed free. "Hand me the bottle of baby oil. It's my turn."

"But..."

"Patience, dear, and turn over."

When he did as she said, grumbling the whole while, she drizzled baby oil in a pool in the small of his back. Straddling him, she then used her femininity to slick the baby oil down over his firm buttocks.

"Uhh...ah...ahhhh..."

"Excuse me?" Alexia said.

"I'm going to die young if you don't stop," Crew groaned as she placed her hands on his shoulders and rubbed her entire body up and down his with slippery suggestion.

"I don't know, you look pretty lively to me," Alexia said with lusty amusement a few seconds later when he rolled to his back, breathing deeply and bracketing his hands behind his head on a pillow.

He lay a few moments, studying her face, which was alive with happy pleasure. Lifting his head finally, he tossed her the pillow he'd been lying back against. "Here, lie over this, I think it's about time I got my closer look at that tattoo of yours."

"You're kidding . . ." Alexia said, staring at the pillow she'd caught.

"Humor me . . ."

Doing just that, she stretched out beside him facedown, slipping the pillow beneath her tummy as he instructed, the act raising her buttocks and displaying the butterfly prominently.

Crew got up and walked around the bed looking at her. "God, you're so beautiful." Pushing aside a drape of mosquito netting, he leaned across the corner of the bed to retrieve the bottle of oil. Kneeling on the bed, he inched her legs apart and then drizzled baby oil down the backs of her thighs.

Forming a V with his hands he ran them up and down her slippery thighs, his thumbs running hot trails of heat just to the juncture of her thighs where he stopped short of her throbbing need, again and again, until she thought she would lose her mind.

He stopped his delicious torture to rain kisses over her quivering bottom, paying special homage to the tiny butterfly tattoo.

Reaching again for the bottle of oil he'd set aside, he upended it, pouring a lazy stream of oil over her cheeks. She could feel it running and pooling in her sloping crevice as she squirmed.

"I want to turn over," Alexia pleaded, looking over her shoulder at Crew, her eyes heavy with desire.

The heat in his own eyes burned hot-feverish, but he admonished, "Not yet . . . not just yet, sweetheart."

It was then he began to knead and squeeze her raised buttocks, edging her passionate ache into a frenzy when he trailed his finger between her cheeks but again stopping short of where she so desperately wanted his touch.

"Ple-ease . . . Crew," she pleaded, looking back over her shoulder.

He nodded and she turned, her hand going to remove the pillow.

"No. Leave it under you," he commanded, settling her bottom on the plump ruffle-edged pillow. Dipping his head he trailed tiny kisses just above her triangle of caramel curls.

Looking up at her, he growled. "You are the sexiest woman on earth. I love your butterfly tattoo. In fact I think you should get another one for me." Using his forefinger he indicated just where.

"Crew!"

"Yeah, guess *I'd* have to learn how to tattoo to allow you to get one there, now wouldn't I?" he agreed, laughing sexily.

"Well then, how 'bout here?" he suggested even more outrageously.

She shook her head, trying not to laugh as he tickled her intimately.

"We'll talk about it later," he decided, reaching again for the baby oil. Using his talented long fingers, he worked the baby oil into her triangle of curls, still continuing to build her ache for him by avoiding touching her where her arching body wanted most to be touched.

The close atmosphere of the netting-draped bed was soon saturated with the heady scent of sex and her curls sheltering her femininity were wet with a mixture of baby oil and her own essence.

"Now, Crew . . . I can't . . ." Alexia begged.

"Very soon," he agreed, pulling her and the pillow beneath her bottom to the very edge of the bed. Kneeling on the floor before her, he poured a pool of baby oil into the palm of his hands and rubbed them together. Parting her legs, he then parted her outer petals exposing the pulse of her throbbing need to him.

He waited a few moments, letting the air and his eyes caress her . . . prolonging and building her desire. Then in the blink of an eye, he lowered his head and pressed his tongue against the pulsating site of her desire, touching off an instantaneous crashing peak of pleasure with its ensuing waves of heavenly completion.

Before she was sated, she felt him rise and enter her, his thrust strong and deep, his own completion brought on by the incredible feel of her contracting velvet smoothness.

"Alexia!" he cried, arching his neck and bowing his body as he shuddered with a pleasure more exquisite than any he had ever imagined.

Minutes later, he carried her back to the top of the bed and lay down beside her. "Did I lie?" he whispered, nuzzling her neck.

She barely had the strength to murmur that, no, he hadn't lied. He'd given her almost unbearable pleasure.

They lay curled in each other's arms contented, too lazy to even talk . . . overwhelmed by the depth of the experience they'd shared. Eventually they dozed off.

It was Alexia who awoke after midnight with a craving for pizza. Creeping out of bed and pulling on a robe, she went to the kitchen.

The aroma of the baking pizza lured Crew from sleep and he joined Alexia as she was taking the pizza out of the oven.

"Were you planning to eat that all by yourself or are you willing to share?" he asked, coming up behind her and nuzzling her neck as she laid the pizza on the counter.

"I think I could be persuaded to share." Alexia chuckled, slapping his hand away from its wicked wanderings.

Crew took the piece of pizza she cut him and sat down on a stool opposite her at the counter.

"You were going to tell me about your misspent youth, remember?" Alexia said, taking a bite of pizza.

"Oh, that."

"You promised," Alexia coaxed.

"I've been on my own for a long time," Crew began, staring off into space. "You see my father died while I was starting high school and my mother remarried."

"You didn't like the man your mother remarried?" Alexia guessed, gauging the expression of dislike on Crew's face.

"He was a jerk."

"Are you sure you didn't like him merely because he took your father's place?"

Crew reached for another piece of pizza. "It wasn't that," he answered honestly. "My stepfather was careful about the image he cultivated around my mother, but he didn't bother with pretense around anyone else, most especially me. He let me know from the start that he didn't want me around. I split as soon as I finished high school."

"Why didn't you try telling your mother... try explaining to her what was going on?"

Crew shrugged. "She was happy."

Alexia finished her second piece of pizza and wiped her hands on a napkin. "I've been on my own since high school, too," she said, wiping the crumbs at her place into a pile.

"Really?" Crew asked, looking up at her.

She nodded. "My family was very poor. Often there wasn't enough food to go around... times I know my parents went to bed hungry so the children could eat. My dresses were patched, as were my shoes... Yours was the first present I've even gotten," she said with a wistful smile.

"Are things better for your family now?" Crew asked.

Tears welled in Alexia's eyes. "My whole family was killed in a house fire shortly after I left. I've been alone in the world since I was nineteen."

"I'm sorry," Crew said, rising and going to her. Lifting her into his arms, he carried her back to bed, comforting her.

Comforting that led to loving. Slow, sweet, lazy lovemaking that drew them back to the kitchen for Swiss chocolate almond ice cream eaten with their fingers amid much creativity.

CREW AND ALEXIA spent the next two evenings readying the hole he'd dug for the tetra liner. After Crew pumped out the rainwater left standing by the storm, Alexia helped him place the old newspapers over the surface of the hole. Sam dozed nearby as they spread the plastic liner, which was made without chemicals that would be harmful to fish.

They worked silently. Alexia didn't seem ready to broach what had happened between them, and Crew decided not to push her... or his luck.

THURSDAY NIGHT everything went to hell in a hand basket. Crew arrived with the order of large stones that would ring the fish pond and anchor the liner. Working steadily at unloading them, he finished by dark, feeling as if his arms were six inches longer from carrying the heavy stones to the fish pond site.

Alexia worked inside going over her presentation for the Funland Amusement Park account. She had an appointment scheduled with the client at three the following day and wanted to be absolutely certain she'd covered any and all angles.

"What are you working on?" Crew asked from the doorway of her bedroom, stopping in to say goodnight.

"The amusement park account," she answered over her shoulder.

"Aren't you ever going to finish it and start mine?"

"It's finished. I'm planning on starting yours tomorrow. I finished this several days ago and I'm just going over it to make sure I didn't overlook anything."

"Was it finished Saturday night when ol' Buttercup came to pick you up?"

"His name is Colby." Alexia sighed. "And, yes, as a matter of fact, it was. Why do you ask?"

"I hope you were smart enough not to show it to him."

Alexia turned in her chair to face Crew. "Of course I showed it to him. Colby is my friend."

Crew snorted. "I wouldn't be so sure."

"What is your problem. Why do you keep insisting on slandering Colby?"

Crew shrugged. "I just don't trust him, that's all. And neither should you."

"Any particular reason other than that *you* don't like him?" she demanded.

Crew leaned into the door frame. "Whether or not I like Colby Langston has nothing to do with it."

"*Really?* And what does?"

He considered her for a moment, then seemed to reach some sort of decision. "You know what we talked about Monday night . . . when I told you about how I, ah . . ."

"Watched me undress?"

"Yes, well, after you got dressed in your workout clothes, there was a knock on your office door, if you remember. You went to answer it. It was Colby, also dressed for the gym."

"We go to the same gym, so? He recommended me for a membership. Rotten of him wasn't it?" she said facetiously.

Crew ignored her remark and continued. "You let Colby into your office and then a few minutes later you left him alone there while you went off on a brief errand of some sort."

"And . . . ?" Alexia said, drumming her fingers on her desk.

"I was about to go back to finishing up washing your window, after all . . ."

"The show was over . . ." Alexia supplied.

She had him speechless for a moment and then he continued. "Before I looked away, something Colby did caught my eye. He started going through your desk."

"So," Alexia said, shrugging. "He was most likely looking for a pen or something."

"In your files, too? I doubt it. No, Colby was looking for something all right. But whatever it was, he didn't want you to know about it. That much was obvious. His search was too stealthy and thorough for that. And when he'd completed his furtive search, he made sure there was no evidence to indicate a search had been conducted."

Alexia leveled a censorious look at Crew.

"I don't believe you."

"Oh, that's rich. You believed my admission about watching you instantly. Why is it you're so willing to believe the worst of me, yet when confronted with something unsavory about Colby Langston, you can't bring yourself to believe it could possibly be true."

"Colby wouldn't do something like that, I'm telling you. He's not the sort . . ."

"What you mean to say is that Colby Langston is your equal and I'm not," Crew bit off, his eyes glowering at her, dark with a mixture of hurt and anger.

"I didn't say that, but Colby comes from a respected family with—"

"That's so much garbage and you know it, Alexia. Being born with a silver spoon in your mouth doesn't make you impervious to human weaknesses. People who have still want more, the same as people who don't have—only their motive is greed, not need. When are you going to realize you're too damn good for the likes of Colby Langston and stop trying so desperately to belong?"

"There's nothing wrong with trying to improve oneself," Alexia said adamantly.

Crew shook his head and looked at her with hopeless frustration as he pushed away from the door frame.

"You just don't get it, do you? This guy is bad news. He's not in your corner. You've got tunnel vision where he's concerned and what's worse is you're a snob. All you think about is *your* life, *your* career."

"Oh, and you don't? You're the one who talked me into giving you advertising for your new company free."

"I did not. I'm building you a fish pond!"

"Then build the damn thing, finish it and get the hell out of my life," Alexia stormed, turning away form him in tears.

"Fine," Crew snapped, fading from her doorway, the kitchen door slamming with hostile finality on his way out.

Dear Editor:

A soft, warm rain is falling here and all I can think of is soft, warm mud. . . and baby oil.

Oh, and I'm thinking of taking my characters to counseling. It's them or me!

Tiffany

11

ALEXIA SAT AT HER DESK in her office Friday morning, idly flipping through a new business magazine that had come in the mail, while sipping a glass of mineral water.

She stopped flipping the pages, an article featuring baby boomers and their new life-styles catching her interest. The article detailed the baby boomers' new stay-at-home cocooning attitude and the shift in taste away from nouvelle cuisine to things like pot roast and mashed potatoes, the comforting foods from childhood. It was in the list of their main concerns that Alexia came up with an idea she could use to promote Crew's new landscaping business.

The environment had headed the list of concerns, and she'd come up with an idea for backyard sanctuaries; environmentally friendly spaces to attract birds, rabbits, chipmunks and yes, however apt, butterflies.

Closing the magazine, Alexia spent the rest of the morning in a frenzy of activity, working up the idea to present to Crew.

The fish pond was very near completion. If she could give him the promised advertising when he finished, he'd be out of her life.

Then she could go back to the orderly pursuit of her goals. There was never any question that Crew Harper was a major distraction. One she didn't need. If the Cheap Thrills Amusement Park presentation went as well as she thought it would later that afternoon, then she'd be within striking distance of a partnership with Gund & Associates, securing her future happiness.

Looking up at the clock, she saw that it was noon. Her stomach churned. Three more hours. If only it were already over. Maybe if she had some lunch . . . She was thinking of doing just that when there was a knock at her office door.

"Did anybody ever tell you you work too hard?"

She looked up to see Eric Challis.

"You know the old saying, all work and no play . . ." he teased.

"Makes me a partner," Alexia finished for him as she stood and offered her hand. "Are you looking for Colby?" she asked.

"Only if you won't go to lunch with me," Eric said smoothly.

"Lunch?"

"You do eat, don't you?" he asked, eyeing the bottle of mineral water on her desk. "You're not one of these women who never eat breakfast or lunch, are you?"

"No." Alexia laughed shortly. "I eat . . . then feel guilty."

"Guilty? What good is guilt?" Eric asked.

Alexia's expression was rueful. "Guilt gets me to the gym."

"Ah, I see. Well, whatever you're doing, it works."

Alexia blushed and looked down at her desk. Shuffling together the papers she had been working on, she stacked them then placed them in a folder on top of the Cheap Thrills Amusement Park presentation.

Eric cleared his throat. "About lunch . . . ?"

Alexia looked up, and hesitated.

"We could talk business . . ."

She didn't say anything as she continued to consider.

" . . . or not," Eric said with a smile.

"I have an appointment with Funland this afternoon, so we can't be gone long," she informed him.

"No problem," he assured her.

"Okay, sure," she agreed, deciding it would make the time go faster and hopefully calm her nerves.

THREE HOURS LATER her nerves were anything but calm.

"How could this possibly have happened?" she cried, pounding her fists in frustration on the wooden door of the restaurant's wine cellar.

She and Eric had had a leisurely lunch in the old-world restaurant filled with antiques and treasures from the owner's extensive travels. Once again, Eric had been greeted on sight and showered with special service.

The black forest cake they'd shared for dessert had been sinfully rich and delicious. Eric had been charming if snobbish company, mocking a few of the restaurant's patrons in hushed tones of condescension.

Crew had called her a snob. It hadn't particularly bothered her at the time, but witnessing the less than admirable attribute in someone else brought home its moral reprehensiveness.

She'd had quite enough of Eric's company by the time they finished lunch with time to spare to make her appointment, but like a moron she'd listened to Eric. He'd insisted they tour the restaurant's famous wine cellar before they left to return to her office.

If only she'd stood her ground and refused, she wouldn't be in the mess she found herself in. Looking at her watch for the hundredth time, she saw another five minutes had passed.

It read three-thirty. She'd blown her appointment with Funland. Showing up late was almost as bad as not showing up at all, which indeed might still be the case if the owner didn't come down soon and let them out.

"I can't believe you left the key in the lock like that," she said, turning to Eric. While they'd been looking at the racks of wine, the door had suddenly swung shut, locking them in, the key ineffectual on the other side of the door.

Eric was nonplussed at her anger as he sat on the floor leaning back against a wine rack with a bottle of vintage wine at his side.

"Why don't you just relax and accept that we're locked in here for the time being. Come join me," he coaxed. "Sooner or later a customer will order wine with dinner and we'll be freed. Until then relax and enjoy the romance of the situation. After all we've got wine," he said, spreading his arms wide, "woman, and given a chance, I'm sure we'd make beautiful music together."

"I do not want to relax," Alexia fumed, "or anything else," she added, glaring at him. "What I want is to get out of here. I'm already late for an important appointment."

Eric waved the bottle of wine in the air dismissing her argument. "Appointments can be rescheduled," he insisted with the cavalier attitude of one who did not have to work for a living.

"Just shut up," Alexia said, finally too frustrated to be bothered reasoning with him.

"Glad to. That is if you'll come on over here and give me something better to do . . ."

"If I come over there what I give you will be a swift kick in the—"

"Never mind then," Eric said with a resigned smile as he slipped his Swiss Army knife from his pocket and used the corkscrew to open the bottle of wine at his side. By his casual attitude, Alexia knew it wasn't the first time Eric had "accidentally" been locked in the wine cellar with his luncheon companion.

"Let us out of here!" she called, pounding on the door.

No one came, but she continued pounding at various intervals throughout the afternoon, to no avail. Eric made no further passes and instead took to singing old college songs as he gradually finished the bottle of wine he'd opened.

By the end of the afternoon Alexia knew two things about Eric: he couldn't carry a tune . . . and he snored.

They weren't released from the wine cellar until six o'clock, too late for Alexia to call Funland and explain at the very least. It would have to wait until Monday.

The ride back to her office was silent. Eric dropped her off at the entrance to the building, glad to be rid of her, it appeared.

Deciding to get some of the wine cellar dust off her, Alexia went into the office building to freshen up before she went home. When she finished freshening up, she went to her office to pick up the folder containing her idea for Crew, planning on taking it home with her so she could finish it.

When she picked up Crew's folder, she saw that the folder with the presentation for the Cheap Thrills Amusement Park wasn't beneath it where she'd left it when she went to lunch. A look of puzzlement crossed her face. She distinctly remembered it being there.

Her tense shoulders relaxed when she realized someone must have come in and moved it when the client had called about her missed appointment.

"Looking for the Cheap Thrills presentation?" Colby asked from the door, coming into her office and taking a seat in the flame-stitched chair near her desk.

Alexia looked up, surprised to see him still there.

"Why? Have you seen it?" she asked.

"I took it."

"What?"

Colby shrugged. "Well, someone had to present it to the client."

"What are you talking about?" she asked, dropping into her chair, feeling as if the rug had been pulled from beneath her feet.

"I presented your proposal to the client," Colby repeated.

"Why? Why didn't you just reschedule?"

Colby arched a brow. "And tell the client you couldn't make it because you were busy in a wine cellar with another client?"

"You could have made up some excuse. It wasn't my fault you know. It was your friend Eric's fault. I still can't believe it happened."

Colby shook his head and looked at her pityingly.

"Wake up and smell the coffee, Alexia."

"What...?" She looked closely at Colby, seeing him in a whole new light. Seeing past the polished manners and patina of sophistication and wealth. "Wait a minute... How did you know about the wine cellar? You set this whole thing up, didn't you? Eric... the wine cellar... everything. You made sure I wouldn't be around to give my presentation to the client, didn't you?"

Colby used his thumb and forefinger to cock an imaginary gun. "That's right."

"But I don't understand... what difference..."

"I presented your idea as my own."

Alexia's mouth dropped open at his betrayal and lack of remorse. She shoved her hand in her hair. "But why? You don't even care about your job here."

Colby rose and began walking toward the door. Pausing in the doorway he turned back to her. "No, that's true. I don't care, but it seems Father does. You see, he's decided he wants me to have a partnership at Gund & Associates and made my getting one part of the conditions of my trust fund."

"That stinks. How could you?"

Colby threw up his hands. "Look at it this way, Alexia. I did you a favor."

"A favor?"

"Yeah, now you know not to trust anyone. Oh, and Alexia, I wouldn't go trying to claim credit for the presentation. It will only make you look like a sore loser... and if it's one thing you don't want to appear, it's a loser."

"Get out."

Alexia sat staring off into space after Colby left her office. She felt like a fool.

And an outsider.

And she didn't like herself very much at the moment, because as painful as it was to acknowledge, it was her own greed, pure and simple that had caused her victimization by someone like Colby.

Sniffing, she took a deep calming breath of determination. She might have been stupid this time, but it wouldn't happen again.

Colby Langston was wrong. She wasn't a loser.

THE FOLLOWING MORNING Alexia was awakened by a wet nose nudging her. She climbed up through the layered fog of sleep. Her eyes blinked open to find Sam sitting beside her, watching her, a ratty looking yellow tennis ball in his mouth. She groaned, lifting her head from the pillow and pushing herself up into a sitting position. Sam whined, then dropped the ball into her lap, wanting her to play.

"You've got to be kidding," Alexia grumbled, rubbing her eyes. It would be at least another half hour before she was conscious, she was sure.

Sunlight streamed in through the panes of the French doors to splash across the foot of her bed, and a heavenly smell was drifting in from the kitchen.

Sam . . . that could only mean Crew was the one rattling pots in the kitchen. She wasn't ready to face him yet, but she had to. She owed him an apology.

She looked over at the clock while Sam swatted her with his paw, trying to get her to play. It was eleven o'clock, she saw. She must have fallen asleep the minute her head had hit the pillow last evening. She remembered bringing Crew's folder home with the intention of doing some work on it, but she hadn't been able to concentrate.

Not after what had happened.

Colby was right.

She couldn't go to her superiors in the firm and complain that Colby had stolen her work and passed it off as his own. It would look as though she was whining, and sour grapes. Especially since they'd both been assigned to the account. Colby had shoved all the work off on her as he usually did, and there was no way to prove what he'd done. She'd lost and had to accept it.

This time.

"S-a-a-m," Crew called from the kitchen.

Sam leaped off the bed and went to his master in the kitchen, but not before retrieving his yellow tennis ball.

Alexia swung her legs over the side of the bed and forced herself to get up and get dressed. When she was dressed in a cropped cotton sweater and white walking shorts, she walked barefoot to the kitchen, her nose following the delicious aromas.

"What are you doing . . . and why?" she asked, taking a stool at the counter as he took a sheet of caramel rolls from the oven.

"I'm cooking your breakfast to celebrate the completion of your fish pond."

"It's finished?"

"Not quite, but it will be by the end of the day. I'm dechlorinating the water and I have to plant the ferns I got last night. Then all that will be left to do is add the fish."

"That reminds me," she said, slipping off the stool and going back to the bedroom. When she returned to the kitchen, she had Crew's folder in her hand. "I came up with an idea to promote your landscaping company. Want to take a look and see what you think?" she asked, handing him the folder.

When he opened the folder, she began her pitch. "I was paging through this magazine, and there was an article on how concerned people are about the environment. So I thought why not do backyard sanctuaries? It ties in with conservation and people's renewed interest in nature. People are staying home more and birdwatching, for example, is becoming popular—that as well as pondscaping and just enjoying wildlife in general."

Crew nodded, looking through the layout she'd sketched. "When did you do this?" he asked.

"Yesterday morning. I had some time before the amusement park presentation, so when I got the idea, I went with it."

"How did the amusement park presentation go?"

"The client loved it. We got the account," Alexia said with a marked lack of enthusiasm as she took a carton of milk from the refrigerator.

Crew watched her pour them both a glass of milk, a puzzled look on his face. "I don't get it. You don't sound happy about your success."

"Did you really make these?" Alexia asked, biting into one of the warm, sticky caramel rolls.

"No, I just warmed them in the oven. I got them at the mall."

"Oh. Well, they're delicious."

"Alexia . . ."

"Hmm . . ."

"What happened?"

She took a drink of the cold milk, then forced herself to look at Crew. "You remember how you kept warning me not to trust Colby Langston?"

Crew nodded, shooing Sam away from a caramel roll he was eyeing.

"Turns out you were right about him," she said. "I should have listened to you."

"What did he do?" Crew asked, his eyes narrowing as he laid the folder she'd given him on the countertop and took a stool across from her.

"He passed my work off as his own. He got the account for the firm, but he did it using my presentation and he took the credit for doing the presentation himself."

"I'm sorry," Crew said, rubbing the back of her hand with his thumb.

"I know losing the amusement park account to Colby was a blow . . . because it was your ticket to security, to belonging."

She nodded. "It's just one more disappointment, but it hurts."

Just then Crew made a swipe at Sam, who still managed to snitch the caramel roll he'd been eyeing. Crew and Alexia both laughed as Sam slunk off to the living room with his booty.

"I hope he doesn't try to bury it in one of your plants," Crew said, pulling the folder toward him and looking at it again. He didn't say anything for a long time as he studied the layout a second time.

Finally he looked up from the folder.

"Well?" she asked nervously.

"I like it." He tapped his finger. "I like it a lot."

"Good, then we're even, right?"

"Even?"

"Our barter arrangement, remember . . . ?"

"Oh, that. Yeah, we're even."

She reached for the folder. "I plan to do some flyers to distribute in targeted neighborhoods, a nice ad in the phone book and maybe a coupon promotion in one of the newspaper ads. I'll put the finishing touches on this so it will be ready for you to take with you when you leave this evening."

"How much are all these things going to cost me? I can't afford much start-up cost, you know."

"I know. We'll start small with the things I'm suggesting, using the neighborhood journals instead of the big newspapers. Word-of-mouth should kick up sales pretty quickly."

"Right."

A long, uncomfortable silence stretched between them, unbroken until Sam came bounding back in, chasing his yellow tennis ball.

"Well, then," Crew said, unfolding his body from the stool. "I have to leave now and take Sam by the vet to have his foot checked. I'll be back later to finish up."

Alexia worked slowly through the morning and the afternoon on the rest of her ideas for Crew's promotion. Subconsciously she didn't want the time she spent with Crew to be over. Late in the afternoon she found herself standing at the kitchen window watching Crew plant the ferns at the edge of the fish pond.

As she watched, she remembered back to the evening he'd driven her to Lone Elk Park. She'd been so furious with him, and he'd put up with her ill-behaved snit. It hadn't been his fault the truck had broken down. She had in fact been nasty to him more often than not. And he'd just kept coming back for more.

Until she'd chosen to believe Colby was the man Crew wasn't. Now Crew was being polite, but distant.

And after today she would probably never see him again.

WHEN CREW FINISHED planting the last of the ferns, he stood and stretched. All that remained to be done was the fish.

On the way back from the vet's, he'd picked up two orange-and-black spotted koi as a surprise for Alexia, and they were floating in plastic bags of water in the middle of the pond so the water temperature would equalize and the fish wouldn't go into shock when he released them.

While Sam barked and splashed his paws in the water trying to help, Crew fished the plastic bags to the side of the pond with a stick and freed the fish into their new home. The colorful pair took off together soaring and diving in the wide expanse of water as Crew and Sam watched.

"Well, Sam, I guess that's it," Crew said, leaning back on his haunches and stroking the dog's neck as the shadows of evening began to descend. "You'd better go dig up your tennis ball where you buried it, so we can go home."

Sam cocked his head intelligently as if trying to remember just where he had buried it and then scampered off in search of it. He returned a few minutes later with the yellow tennis ball, barely distinguishable because it was covered in wet sand. Sam had buried it in a little kid's sandbox next door.

Both Sam and Crew looked to the back door when they heard it open. Alexia walked outside, heading toward them with Crew's folder in her hand.

"Okay, this is it," Crew said, patting Sam's head. "Pretend you're going to miss her, boy."

Sam barked several times in comment.

"Shut up, Sam," Crew said, beginning to gather the spades and buckets into the wheelbarrow, preparing to load everything into the truck.

"You've done a beautiful job," Alexia said as she approached the fish pond. When she reached it, a spotted koi splashed in the water, catching her attention as it swam beneath a pink blossoming water lily.

"What was that?" she asked as both koi came swimming back into view.

"That's Grant and Lee... I thought I'd give you something to remember me by... the Civil War... always battling..."

Enemies? Is that what they were at last?

And she'd almost been about to beg him not to go. She wanted him to grin at her... to make everything all better with his special knack of fun and charm. She wanted to tell him that she loved him, when frankly my dear, he didn't give a damn, she thought, watching a koi swim by her feet. She wondered absently if it was her namesake, Grant. Unlike that other Grant, she wasn't going to win this war.

"I guess the pond is finished," she said, handing him the folder containing her completed advertising promotion for his landscaping firm.

"Yes, and I guess we are, too," Crew replied, taking the folder from her.

Alexia stuck out her hand. "I wish you every success with your new landscaping venture," she said.

Crew took her offered hand. "I know your career is important to you," he said. "I'm sorry about what happened."

Alexia shrugged. "I'll win next time."

Crew nodded.

"Come on, Sam," Crew said, taking up the wheelbarrow. Sam jumped in for a free ride.

Alexia smiled at Sam's antics. She was even going to miss him...wet nose, fangs, shabby tennis ball and all. Her eyes teared as she watched Crew's retreating back.

At the last minute he turned, his slick grin in place, a glint of mischief in his eyes. Ever the gambler, he couldn't resist taking one last chance.

"You know," he said, "a brook would go nice with the fish pond . . . maybe a little waterfall . . . some wooden benches . . . a hammock . . . an old-fashioned gazebo . . ."

Alexia groaned. "I've got a feeling this pondscape could go on forever. . . ."

"Funny," Crew said. "I had the same feeling about us."

"What do you mean?"

His hands rose to his hips. "You drive me crazy. . . in every way," he vowed. "I'm crazy in love with you." His long legs ate up the distance between them. Reaching her, he took her in his arms, his lips brushing hers. "Alexia, will you marry me?"

Sam bounded from the wheelbarrow and began barking, running in excited circles around them.

Alexia pulled back away form him. "You are crazy. I can't marry you. I hardly know you. I don't even know where you live."

"I live in a trailer in Sunset Hills, the first one on your left as you drive past the motel."

"It's not just that. Sure you're fun and we have a good time together, but you have no ambition, no drive. You live your life in a devil-may-care manner without any plan for the future."

"I have plans. What about the landscaping business?"

"You know as well as I do that it's just a lark to you."

"I could make it work," he objected.

"Yes, you could. But would you? I don't think so. I don't think you can commit yourself to anything. Marriage is a big commitment, Crew. You don't really want to marry me."

His eyes were wounded but his voice was angry when he answered her, "I don't know what I must have been thinking of. You're right, now that I think about it, I *don't* want to marry you. I don't want to marry someone who's as confused as you are about who she is. You're so wrapped up in your yuppie life-style, you refuse to allow yourself fun, the love of a real man..." Sam whined at his feet. "Or even a pet. Come on, Sam, let's go. We're not wanted here."

Dear Editor:

Crew and Alexia still aren't cooperating. So far this is turning out to be a story about a man and his dog, maybe I could interest Disney...

Is the rule about happy endings a hard and fast one? Better cross your fingers, I've only got the next chapter to pull it off . . .

Tiffany

12

ALEXIA STEWED FOR DAYS, first hurt, then angry over Crew's harsh words when he'd retracted his marriage proposal. Still, in the end, she'd come to realize he'd spoken the truth. She *was* sacrificing too much of herself to get what she wanted. But all that was going to change, and tonight was as good a time as any to start, she vowed, rifling through her closet for just the right outfit.

Her hand came to rest on a pair of shiny black biker pants she'd bought on impulse and never worn. Yeah, tonight called for spandex, she decided, yanking the pants from the hanger and wriggling into them. Rummaging in the bottom of her closet she came up with her black high tops. The dresser drawer yielded a pair of neon-yellow socks.

Pulling them on, she wondered what to wear for a top. It had to be sexy and outrageous. She thought a moment, then came up with the idea of using a black-and-yellow kerchief, wrapping it bandeau style, defying the laws of gravity.

Bending from the waist, she brushed out her hair after adding a spritz of mousse. Standing, she shook her head once and let her curls settle in a wild array around her face.

From her jewelry box, she took a pair of oversize silver hoops, slipping them into her pierced ears and added a charm bracelet made up of bottle caps to her wrist.

Going into the bathroom, she did her makeup, paying particular attention to her eyes. The finishing touch was the red, red lipstick she slicked on her pouty lips.

One more thing and she'd be ready. Searching through her medicine chest, she came up with bright red nail polish to match her lips.

It was eight o'clock by the time she'd located Crew's trailer and began pounding on the door.

She could hear Sam barking on the other side, and then Crew's "Keep your pants on, I'm coming" as she continued to pound.

The door swung open a minute later.

"I must be dreaming," Crew said, his jaw dropping when he saw her getup. When she started to say something, he raised his hand to stop. "No, don't wake me. I like this dream a hell of a lot," he said, his eyes sweeping over her.

"I've come to apologize," she said.

"It keeps getting better," he said, leaning into the door.

"Can I come in?" she asked, looking around him at Sam, who was sitting down thumping his tail happily.

"I guess," Crew said, moving aside.

When she was inside, Crew opened a cabinet door and took out a rawhide bone almost as big as Sam. "Here, boy, this ought to keep you occupied. Go watch TV."

Sam carried the rawhide bone to the couch, his disregard for them immediate.

Alexia glanced around the inside of Crew's trailer. "You're a bit of a collector, aren't you?" she said, taking in the organized chaos.

"Yeah, I tend to get attached to things when I really like them."

"I don't know. You let me go pretty easily," she said.

"It didn't seem easy to me."

"Do you think we could try again?" she asked.

"What about our differences?" he hedged, wanting to try, yet still hurt by her rejection.

"Maybe we can learn from each other. Maybe I can inspire you to take your future seriously, and you can get me to relax and have fun, instead of being such a stick-in-the-mud."

"Sounds like a good idea to me."

"So how about a date," she asked boldly.

"A date?"

"Yeah, I thought you might want to be there when I loosen up. I want to go back to the amusement park with you. I've always had this secret fantasy about roller coasters."

"Hot damn. You're on your own, Sam," Crew said, reaching for his keys.

Crew could hardly take his eyes off her as he drove them to the amusement park. "One condition," he said, parking the truck when they got there.

"What's that?"

"No visit to see the fortune teller, okay? She was wrong about you being a partner anyway."

"Agreed," Alexia said, jumping down from the truck, "but only if we don't go see Miss D Cup Bangles dance again, either."

Crew made a pretense of hesitating, then laughed and agreed.

Taking her hand after he paid their way in he asked, "So what's the deal with the roller coaster?"

"You'll see," she said as he led her toward it.

"Hmm...well, at any rate, I must say I like how you dress for a bonafide date."

"So do I," Alexia agreed, pleased with herself for giving in to her sometimes exotic tastes.

"I'll get the tickets," Crew said when they reached the roller coaster ride, aptly called, he thought, The Rickety Rocket.

Her hand stayed his. "No . . . this is my treat."

He stood looking at the old monstrosity while she stood in line for tickets. It looked like a piece of bleached-out driftwood. He didn't want to even think about how old it was. No one in their right mind would ride on that death trap, he thought, then admitted to himself he hadn't been in his right mind since he'd first laid eyes on Alexia.

Tickets in hand, she tugged him toward the very first car of the train. Wonderful, he thought, he'd be able to see death coming to greet him.

When everyone was seated in the train, it jerked and took off. The train wandered around the circle and then began its slow chugging rise up the incline of shuddering wooden tracks.

Crew looked over at Alexia. Her face was lit with excitement, a pale glow showing through her light tan. Her eyes were dancing with anticipation.

The train seemed to be going even slower as it neared the top, teasing with what lay just ahead. It inched closer and closer to the peak and then suddenly it was over the top and descending with maddening speed. The wind rushed by his ears and caught his breath. The bottom fell out of his stomach.

Oh, no, he was going to be sick! And then he was okay again as the train settled into a nice easy ride until it would begin to climb again.

Crew looked over at Alexia. There was a thin sheen of perspiration on her upper lip. Her cheeks were flushed and her eyes sparkled. All at once he saw the sexuality of the roller coaster ride; there was the slow buildup, the steady climb of anticipation, then the peak, followed by the catch-your-breath plummet.

The ride went over a few lesser dips and then the train began to slow as it pulled near the boarding platform. *Thank God!* He'd managed to make it through one ride without the motion sickness overcoming him.

He was about to get out of the train when Alexia reached across him and handed more tickets to the attendant. She looked at him with feigned innocence, and said, "One ride doesn't satisfy me. I bought several tickets."

Crew hoped his luck held as the big hill loomed ahead of them. What the heck, he decided. He had nothing to lose but his lunch. He slid his arm along the back of the car, and when they reached the summit of the hill, he planted his lips on Alexia's neck and closed his eyes. He didn't know if her racing pulse beneath his lips was due to him or the ride, but he knew it was the most incredible sensation, and all thought of motion sickness slipped from his mind.

Rise and plummet, rise and plummet...and she could do little more than squirm. He loved it.

"Well, what do you think?" Crew asked as they neared the boarding platform after their final ride. His eyes were dancing. "Was that the best ride you've ever had in your life, or what...?"

"Crew...?"

"Hmm...?"

"Will you marry me?"

"I thought you'd never ask," he said, pulling her into his arms. "Let's go back to my place and practice the honeymoon."

Alexia laughed. "You're b-a-d."

Crew winked. "That's why I need practice."

"NOW FOR THE FUN PART," Crew said, setting Alexia down after carrying her over the threshold of their room at the Claymont Inn, "Unwrapping you."

Instead of choosing a floral bouquet for their wedding at City Hall, Alexia had elected to wear a twice-wrapped necklace of sweet peas, blue lace and campanula above her strapless gown from Creative Illusions, its bodice inset with bits of lace and narrow lengths of satiny white ribbon. Crew leaned as close as he could, what with the drifting yards of white tulle making up the skirt of her wedding dress, and with the fragrance of her necklace flaring his nostrils, bestowed a series of nibbling kisses across her lush cleavage. Kisses that sent shivers of delight all the way to her toes, which curled in response inside her white pumps.

"Don't I get to unwrap *you*?" she asked, her hands tugging playfully at the tooled silver heart catch of the bolo tie he'd worn with his tuxedo.

"But I've got first dibs," he objected, marshaling a sexy pout.

"So sue me," she answered, grinning up at him as she crowded him back against the wall and popped the studs of his tuxedo shirt. Slipping her hands inside, she rubbed the planes and hollows of his well-muscled chest, feeling his accelerated heartbeat. She pushed his starched white shirt open, tugging it from his pants, the scent of warm male and after-shave enticing her to lean in and bite, openmouthed, at the curve of his neck and shoulder.

"You're an animal...." he growled, pulling down the top of her strapless gown and filling his palms with her spilling breasts, kneading and squeezing gently.

She bit him, raking her teeth down his shoulder, inching up the sensual tension.

"We have a bed . . ." he gasped, when her teeth raked over his nipple and her hand brushed fleetingly over the fly of his pants.

"Ummm . . ." She moaned, looking down to see his dark hands, the gold wedding band cool against her creamy white breasts.

Her eyes fluttered closed, and he fitted his mouth to hers, thrusting his tongue past her maddening teeth to explore and plunder. Their heavy breathing and her rustling gown were the only sounds in the room.

She pushed his jacket down his shoulders and it fell to the floor.

"Aren't I supposed to retrieve a garter or something?" Crew murmured against her lips.

"Ummm..."

He two-stepped her over to the bed, both of them nibbling at each other's lips the whole way. She sat on the edge of the bed and Crew knelt before her to begin lifting the layer after layer of white tulle, while Alexia leaned back on her elbows, a secret smile on her face, a warm sensual languor in her eyes.

"Ah-ha..." Crew said at last, getting to the end of the layers of tulle to find white lace stockings, and as he explored upward matching garters of ruffled lace trimmed in streamers of narrow pink ribbon. Some layers of tulle drifted down. When he shoved them back up, his hand brushed her soft downy mound.

"Alexia...!" he said, his eyes wide.

"Surprise..."

"But Alexia..."

"Why, Mr. Harper. I do believe you're shocked."

"I'm certainly ah...um..."

"Y-e-s..."

"You're b-a-d, Mrs. Harper..."

"So what are you going to do about it, Mr. Harper...spank me?"

Crew's grin was lethal. "Capital idea...Mrs. Harper..."

COLBY LANGSTON SAT at his desk at Gund & Associates trying desperately to come up with an idea, any idea. He'd been sitting there for long fruitless hours. No matter how hard he tried, he just wasn't creative.

And the worst of it was he still hadn't gotten the partnership or his trust. Gund & Associates had come up with some song and dance about profits being off and now not being the right time to take on another partner.

Giving up the string of paperclips he was making, Colby got up and went to the window to pull the drapes and let in some light.

The sight that greeted him made his stomach churn.

How could Alexia have given up her good job to join forces with Crew Harper, he wondered, staring out the window of his fourth-floor office at the couple lost in an embrace on the window-washing scaffolding. Colby couldn't believe the small size of the diamond twinkling on her finger; it couldn't be more than a carat.

But that wasn't the worst of it.

The worst of it was they looked so disgustingly happy.

Epilogue

ALEXIA PACED back and forth. Crew was late. Again. The dinner she'd prepared was getting cold. Again. In a snit, she took the chocolate cake she'd made him from scratch and fed it piece by piece to the garbage disposal, licking bits of fudge frosting from her fingertips as she did so. Chocolate always made her feel better.

And she definitely needed to feel better.

When she'd married Crew Harper, she'd never imagined he had the capacity to be more of a workaholic than she'd ever been. Imagined that he'd actually choose work over play... that he'd... that he'd, she sniffed, choose work over... over her!

He kept explaining it was only temporary, just until they got their fledgling landscaping business off the ground, and she believed him. But she couldn't help feeling the way she felt.

She wasn't a child. She knew starting a new business took a lot of sacrifice and work. And she'd done her share working right alongside Crew. It was only that he'd gone overboard, focusing on starting up the business to the exclusion of everything else. She missed the fun. She missed *him*.

And she didn't have a clue where his sudden penchant for wearing suits had come from. While there was no danger of his turning into Colby Langston, she rather missed his snug and faded ragged jeans, his irreverent T-shirts. Most of all she missed his irresponsible charm. Was she being selfish to feel neglected because he worked so hard and long? Probably, but that didn't stop her from feeling that way.

Hearing his key in the lock, and Sam's happy bark, she quickly brushed the last of the cake crumbs into the sink and washed them down the drain.

"Hi, fella, look what I brought you...leftover pizza. Now be a good boy and stay, okay?"

"Alexia?" When there was no answer he went in search of her.

"Ummm... what smells so good?" he asked, sniffing the air as he entered the kitchen, setting his black briefcase on a kitchen chair, then bussing Alexia's cheek with a kiss of hello.

"It *was* chocolate cake..."

"Was? Oh, I get it. You're upset with me because I'm a little late."

"Two hours is not a little late."

"Two hours?" he glanced down at his watch. "Ouch, you're right. I'm really sorry, sweetheart. Look, I've got great news, though." Loosening his striped tie, he opened the briefcase he'd set on the chair and withdrew some papers that looked impressively important.

"What's that?" Alexia asked, her interest caught despite her earlier anger.

He handed the papers to her and she began scanning them.

"Crew, this is a contract!"

"That's right."

"But this means . . ."

"Exactly. Now we won't have to do windows anymore. With this contract Harper Environs is in business full-time. No more scaffolding to hang from. From now on we'll—"

"But how did you get this contract?"

Crew shrugged. "It was simple."

"Simple? Crew, contracts this size are not simple to get. How did you get it?"

He threw up his hands. "All I did was talk to your old buddy Buttercup. After our little *talk*, he recommended the idea of landscaping the Cheap Thrills Amusement Park as an addendum to Gund's proposal, recommending Harper Environs as the company to do the work. Cheap Thrills went for it and we got the job."

"Just like that."

"Piece of cake," Crew answered, grinning wickedly.

"Crew . . ."

"So I leaned on Buttercup a little."

"You didn't!" she said, her eyes wide. "You did."

"So now do I get a piece of chocolate cake as my reward or did you throw it all down the disposal again?"

Alexia looked sheepish.

"You did. What did I tell you about doing that?" A dangerous glint surfaced in his eyes. "You know that only leaves one option . . ."

"What?" she asked, slowly backing away.

"You know what. There's only one other thing you make from scratch."

"Crew, dinner's getting cold."

"It's already cold. And I'm already hot . . ."

"Crew, I spent hours on dinner."

"So you're the one who insists on being domestic. I never insisted you cook all these meals that are always cold by the time I make it home."

"But I thought you'd want . . ."

Crew reached to pull her into his arms. "What I want is for you to be happy. . . ."

"Then quit wearing suits at every opportunity," Alexia said, undoing the top button of his starched shirt.

"But I thought that's what you'd want . . ."

She put her finger to his lips, stilling him. "What I want is for you to be happy. . . ."

"Hmm. . . that brings us back to that other thing you make from scratch," he said, lifting her onto the kitchen table with a devilish gleam in his eyes.

"The kitchen table . . . Crew, you're not serious!"

"That's right, I've given up being serious," he answered, beginning to undo his tie. "You see my partner doesn't like me being serious all the time. Remember Madam Rose . . . she was right after all, you did wind up being a partner."

Alexia affected a sultry pout. "Is that what we are . . . partners?" she asked, watching as he tugged off his suit jacket, shirt and tie.

"In every way," he murmured, his hand slipping up her skirt.

It wasn't until some time later that Alexia discovered what Crew had up his sleeve... the reason he'd been two hours late...

A tattoo on his bicep in the shape of a heart.

Inside the heart one word was stenciled.

Taken

Dear Editor:

I had this dream last night... at least I think it was a dream... that I went to this tattoo parlor to do some research for Cheap Thrills.

In the dream the tattoo artist wasn't this retired old salt with gray whiskers. No, this tattoo parlor had three, count 'em three, tattoo artists on the premises. Three gorgeous guys, all of them in choker whites wanting to tattoo me.

The funny thing is when I woke up this morning, I found these three tiny tattoos on my... never mind. Do you think... Nah.

Tiffany

You'll flip . . . your pages won't!
Read paperbacks *hands-free* with

Book Mate • I

The perfect "mate" for all your romance paperbacks

Traveling • Vacationing • At Work • In Bed • Studying • Cooking • Eating

Perfect size for all standard paperbacks, this wonderful invention makes reading a pure pleasure! Ingenious design holds paperback books OPEN and FLAT so even wind can't ruffle pages – leaves your hands free to do other things. Reinforced, wipe-clean vinyl-covered holder flexes to let you turn pages without undoing the strap... supports paperbacks so well, they have the strength of hardcovers!

Pages turn WITHOUT opening the strap.

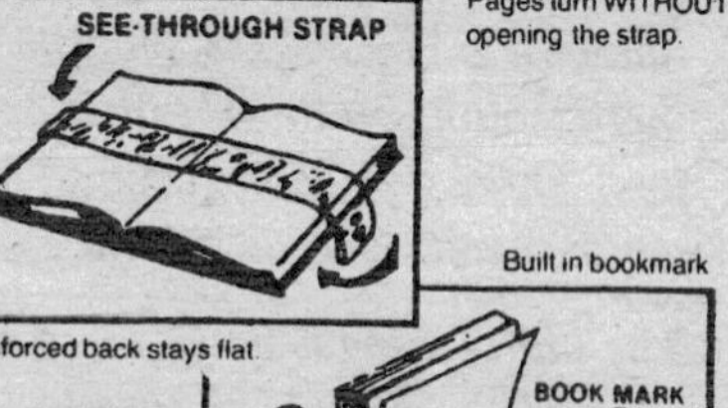

Built in bookmark

Reinforced back stays flat.

BOOK MARK

BACK COVER HOLDING STRIP

10" x 7¼", opened.
Snaps closed for easy carrying, too.

Available now. Send your name, address, and zip code, along with a check or money order for just $5.95 + .75¢ for delivery (for a total of $6.70) payable to Reader Service to:

Reader Service
Bookmate Offer
3010 Walden Avenue
P.O. Box 1396
Buffalo, N.Y. 14269-1396

Offer not available in Canada
***New York residents add appropriate sales tax.**

BM-GR

PASSPORT TO ROMANCE VACATION SWEEPSTAKES

OFFICIAL RULES

SWEEPSTAKES RULES AND REGULATIONS. NO PURCHASE NECESSARY.

HOW TO ENTER:

1. To enter, complete this official entry form and return with your invoice in the envelope provided, or print your name, address, telephone number and age on a plain piece of paper and mail to: Passport to Romance, P.O. Box #1397, Buffalo, N.Y. 14269-1397. No mechanically reproduced entries accepted.
2. All entries must be received by the Contest Closing Date, midnight, December 31, 1990 to be eligible.
3. Prizes: There will be ten (10) Grand Prizes awarded, each consisting of a choice of a trip for two people to: i) London, England (approximate retail value $5,050 U.S.); ii) England, Wales and Scotland (approximate retail value $6,400 U.S.); iii) Caribbean Cruise (approximate retail value $7,300 U.S.); iv) Hawaii (approximate retail value $ 9,550 U.S.); v) Greek Island Cruise in the Mediterranean (approximate retail value $12,250 U.S.); vi) France (approximate retail value $7,300 U.S.).
4. Any winner may choose to receive any trip or a cash alternative prize of $5,000.00 U.S. in lieu of the trip.
5. Odds of winning depend on number of entries received.
6. A random draw will be made by Nielsen Promotion Services, an independent judging organization on January 29, 1991, in Buffalo, N.Y., at 11:30 a.m. from all eligible entries received on or before the Contest Closing Date. Any Canadian entrants who are selected must correctly answer a time-limited, mathematical skill-testing question in order to win. Quebec residents may submit any litigation respecting the conduct and awarding of a prize in this contest to the Régie des loteries et courses du Quebec.
7. Full contest rules may be obtained by sending a stamped, self-addressed envelope to: "Passport to Romance Rules Request", P.O. Box 9998, Saint John, New Brunswick, E2L 4N4.
8. Payment of taxes other than air and hotel taxes is the sole responsibility of the winner.
9. Void where prohibited by law.

PASSPORT TO ROMANCE VACATION SWEEPSTAKES

OFFICIAL RULES

SWEEPSTAKES RULES AND REGULATIONS. NO PURCHASE NECESSARY.

HOW TO ENTER:

1. To enter, complete this official entry form and return with your invoice in the envelope provided, or print your name, address, telephone number and age on a plain piece of paper and mail to: Passport to Romance, P.O. Box #1397, Buffalo, N.Y. 14269-1397. No mechanically reproduced entries accepted.
2. All entries must be received by the Contest Closing Date, midnight, December 31, 1990 to be eligible.
3. Prizes: There will be ten (10) Grand Prizes awarded, each consisting of a choice of a trip for two people to: i) London, England (approximate retail value $5,050 U.S.); ii) England, Wales and Scotland (approximate retail value $6,400 U.S.); iii) Caribbean Cruise (approximate retail value $7,300 U.S.); iv) Hawaii (approximate retail value $ 9,550 U.S.); v) Greek Island Cruise in the Mediterranean (approximate retail value $12,250 U.S.); vi) France (approximate retail value $7,300 U.S.).
4. Any winner may choose to receive any trip or a cash alternative prize of $5,000.00 U.S. in lieu of the trip.
5. Odds of winning depend on number of entries received.
6. A random draw will be made by Nielsen Promotion Services, an independent judging organization on January 29, 1991, in Buffalo, N.Y., at 11:30 a.m. from all eligible entries received on or before the Contest Closing Date. Any Canadian entrants who are selected must correctly answer a time-limited, mathematical skill-testing question in order to win. Quebec residents may submit any litigation respecting the conduct and awarding of a prize in this contest to the Régie des loteries et courses du Quebec.
7. Full contest rules may be obtained by sending a stamped, self-addressed envelope to: "Passport to Romance Rules Request", P.O. Box 9998, Saint John, New Brunswick, E2L 4N4.
8. Payment of taxes other than air and hotel taxes is the sole responsibility of the winner.
9. Void where prohibited by law.

PASSPORT TO ROMANCE
WIN 1 of 10 Vacations SEE INSIDE

VACATION SWEEPSTAKES

MONTH 2 ENTRY

Official Entry Form

Yes, enter me in the drawing for one of ten Vacations-for-Two! If I'm a winner, I'll get my choice of any of the six different destinations being offered — and I won't have to decide until after I'm notified!

Return entries with invoice in envelope provided along with Daily Travel Allowance Voucher. Each book in your shipment has two entry forms — and the more you enter, the better your chance of winning!

Name ____________________

Address ____________________ Apt. ______

City ____________ State/Prov. ____________ Zip/Postal Code ____________

Daytime phone number ____________________
Area Code

☐ I am enclosing a Daily Travel Allowance Voucher in the amount of $__________ Write in amount revealed beneath scratch-off

- - - - - - - - - - - - - - - - - - - -

PASSPORT TO ROMANCE
WIN 1 of 10 Vacations SEE INSIDE

VACATION SWEEPSTAKES

MONTH 2 ENTRY

Official Entry Form

Yes, enter me in the drawing for one of ten Vacations-for-Two! If I'm a winner, I'll get my choice of any of the six different destinations being offered — and I won't have to decide until after I'm notified!

Return entries with invoice in envelope provided along with Daily Travel Allowance Voucher. Each book in your shipment has two entry forms — and the more you enter, the better your chance of winning!

Name ____________________

Address ____________________ Apt. ______

City ____________ State/Prov. ____________ Zip/Postal Code ____________

Daytime phone number ____________________
Area Code

☐ I am enclosing a Daily Travel Allowance Voucher in the amount of $__________ Write in amount revealed beneath scratch-off

CPS-TWO